ALL IN
IS HA.

E.M. Phillips

A SEQUEL TO
'RETURN TO FALCON FIELD'

'Love is not changed by death,

And nothing is lost

And all in the end is Harvest.'

Edith Sitwell

This one is for

Richard B. Purdue

Who launched book 1 into print

Encouraged me all the way to book 10

And in the process become a much valued friend.

Thank you, Dick

Acknowledgement and thanks to:

James Reeves: Cover Photo

David Dempsey: Cover design

Dick Purdue at Indian Lake, NY
for Editing and (again) checking my American 'voice'

ALL IN THE END IS HARVEST

E.M. Phillips

All in the end is harvest

Published 2014 by Sagittarius Publications
62 Jacklyns Lane, Alresford, Hampshire SO24 9LH
Tel: 01962 734322

Typeset by John Owen Smith

ISBN 978-0-9555778-9-5

Printed and bound by CPI Group (UK) Ltd, Croydon, CR0 4YY

PART ONE

1957–1966

IN THE BEGINING

'I remember, I remember, the house where I was born…'

Thomas Hood

CHAPTER 1

Hawksley Manor, Hampshire, December 1957

It was the week before her thirteenth birthday that Sophie first found the photograph album.

She'd spent the morning combing each room in the entire house for evidence that her father had bought her the *Picture Show Annual of 1957,* essential reading if she was to keep up with the rest of her year when she returned to school in January. Although Geoffrey had hinted that *Swallows & Amazons* was a more suitable birthday gift for a girl of her age, rather than cover-to-cover gossip with pictures of David Niven, Elizabeth Taylor (with yet *another* husband), Marlon Brando, Rita Hayworth, and a myriad more impossibly handsome and beautiful Film Stars. It wasn't that Sophie really minded; birthdays were always exciting, no matter if you didn't get your heart's desire, but she *would* like to know for certain...

But by midday, however thorough her search, she still hadn't found the octavo-size, gift-wrapped parcel that would signal success. Very soon her father and Pru – that most wonderful person, who had suddenly appeared almost two years ago to become their housekeeper, thus saving father and daughter from the clutches of the dozen or more bossy nurses who had come and gone in quick succession since the accident – would be back from Geoffrey's regular three-monthly visit to the hospital. For a few moments Sophie stood indecisive, wondering if she was desperate enough to actually *search* the room at the end of the long upper corridor; the room that had been Rupert's and was still somehow filled with his presence.

Suddenly the need to know if the *Picture Show Annual* had made it over Arthur Ransome was too strong to resist and she *had* looked simply everywhere else ... it was her last chance. Taking a deep breath, Sophie marched towards the door which still held a sheet of bilious yellow cardboard with the schoolboy warning printed beneath a drawing of the skull and crossbones:

PRIVATE
KEEP OUT ON PAIN OF DEATH!

She turned the handle gently, as she always did on those rare occasions when the need to cross that threshold into the past became overwhelming; then she would sit in the small cretonne-covered chair by the window and let the memories crowd in on her: memories still so immediate and painful that entering felt at first like an intrusion into Rupert's private world.

She knew it would be as it always was; just as it had been that bright July day three years before, when she had helped her mother make it ready with clean bed linen and towels. Only the vase of wild flowers would be missing.

It had been such a special day. At eighteen, Rupert was leaving school for good to spend the whole long summer at home, before Oxford and his entry into the wide world beyond the schoolroom.

For perhaps a full minute Sophie stood quite still, letting the silence close around her, almost expecting to see him, as she had so many times in the past, hunched over his desk, painstakingly cutting and gluing balsa or plastic, creating yet another 'plane to join those already hanging from the ceiling. See him turn in his chair; hear him ask, "Hi, kid, what is it you want now?"

She took another deep breath; for heaven's sake she was no longer a kid, very soon she would be a *teenager*...swiftly she closed the door behind her and did something she had never ventured to do before; she began a methodical search of the desk. Her father would not have thought of such a hiding place, but Pru, or Mrs Buckley, just might...

Disturbed by the draught from the closing door, Spitfire, Hurricane, Mosquito and a half-dozen other aircraft swung gently above her head as she crouched before the desk and began opening one drawer after another, lifting with care papers and aircraft magazines and old schoolbooks, hoping, but not really expecting, to find the parcel on which she had pinned her hopes.

Then, at the very bottom of the last drawer, beneath a pile of LIFE magazines with pictures of Churchill, and a copy of the Daily Mail, the headline proclaiming: '**VE DAY – IT'S ALL OVER**,' she found a thick, square album of photographs.

Sophie sat on the floor, her back against the desk and balancing the album on her knees opened the worn red cover. In round carefully formed writing she read aloud:

'This photograph album belongs to
Rupert Hamilton de Lacy
Hawksley Manor
Hampshire
England

The World
The Universe
Outer Space'

Gosh, she thought, he must have been a lot younger than she was now when he wrote that!

It wasn't really a proper album; just a quarto scrapbook, of thick grey paper between red fabric covers. On every page were pasted one or more photographs, the captions beneath each written in the same rounded hand.

The book was full, with pictures of her mother and grandmother; of Mrs Buckley and Nanny Elgin, who had been first Rupert's nanny, then Sophie's until she was seven, photographs too, of Old Elias, dead some eight years, and whom she could only dimly remember, together with those of his two sons, young Eli and Tom, teenagers then, who still worked the farm and whom Sophie had known all her life; a half-dozen of Rupert's Labrador, Gunner ...and pictures too, lots of them, of a tall, fair-haired stranger in American uniform, who had the lean, polished looks of a film star and wore silver pilot's wings on his breast; an individual she didn't recognize, whose pictures Rupert had labelled, "Captain Pop" – an odd sort of name, she thought, for a man who looked like a film star. This Captain Pop was on almost every page: astride Sampson, her father's black hunter, with Rupert perched on the saddle before him, a look of pride mingled with apprehension on her brother's face; standing beside their mother at the gate in the big field; seated under the chestnut tree with the older Mrs de Lacy...image after image of Captain Pop – all with *her* mother, *her* brother, *her* grandmother, *her* Tom and Eli...

She closed the album slowly. Now who on earth, she mused, was Captain Pop – and what had he been doing making himself so free with the de Lacy family...and why were there no pictures of her father?

As she closed the album she saw at bottom of the cover, printed in capital letters, in an older version of Rupert's childish hand, the stark message:

IN MEMORY OF MY CAPTAIN POP
KILLED IN ACTION 1944.

She let her hand rest on the few sad words: nineteen forty-four: well, she hadn't been born until December of that year, so couldn't possibly ever have met Rupert's Captain Pop.

And yet there was something about that face in the old black and white photographs that was tantalisingly familiar...the distinctive flaxen hair and sculptured features, the long eyes and the way one corner of his mouth lifted just a little higher than the other when he smiled...

She wondered why Rupert hadn't ever shown her his album, because he'd never been like some of her friend's older brothers, who wanted nothing to do with their sisters. Rupert had shared lots of secrets with her – about what he got up to at school; the air pistol he'd bought from Jimmy Rutherford in the village and kept hidden in his sports kit; how he wasn't going do as dad wanted and be a soldier like all the other de Lacy's; that no matter how much dad hollered, he was going to join the Air Force the minute he could, and fly aeroplanes for the rest of his life...oh, if *only* she had found the album before Rupert died; if she'd asked him, or even mummy or granny; surely *someone* would have told her who Captain Pop was?

Reluctantly, she placed the album back under the newspapers, some instinct telling her that she shouldn't mention finding it to any one, not even her dad, who hated to talk about anything to do with the war. Anyway, Captain Pop was probably dead by the time her father came home from North Africa...no, she decided, the album should stay a secret forever and ever, a secret between Rupert and her and nobody else. Most probably no one else knew about it; even her father; it *had* been well hidden and he was not a man to pry.

But it was a hard secret to keep, and several times in the weeks that followed she almost confided in Pru, who was the loveliest and best of confidents, but then that would seem disloyal to her father, so she kept quiet, but did creep back from time to time and leaf through the album again; always with a growing sense that the unknown Captain Pop had been someone treasured and special in her brother's life.

Her father did buy her 'Swallows and Amazons' for her birthday, but thanks to Pru she also got the coveted Picture Show Annual as well, which Pru had kept hidden in a drawer in her own apartments, where she knew Sophie would never have thought to look.

* * *

It was about this time when she was about to enter the turbulent years of adolescence, that Sophie began to realise the important part Pru played in their lives. When she had first came to Hawksley she was in her late forties, a widow, whose husband had been killed in the Normandy landings. She had no children and had lived alone until her

10

younger brother contracted polio. When he was finally released from the hospital she had taken him home and nursed him through the few months before his death, so she knew all about the loss of love.

She'd slipped so easily into Sophie's life, and had brought Geoffrey de Lacy back from the very edge of despair, to become again, mentally, if not physically, the man he had been before the accident. In the same easy, quiet way, she had encouraged a very sad and withdrawn child to once again find the world a safe and exciting place to be. With her small, trim figure, clear, regular features, soft brown hair and sparkling blue eyes, Sophie thought her beautiful, and although he never said so, and she never once saw him show Pru anything other than an affectionate respect, she was pretty sure her father thought her beautiful too, and wove a few fanciful pubescent dreams about the pair of them, in which she was a demure and enchanting bridesmaid at their nuptials in the village church.

But of course, when she became a proper teenager and knew all about the facts of life, most of them inaccurate and gleaned from her more sophisticated school friends, she went off the bridesmaid fantasy. The very idea of her father and Pru doing such things was quite out of the question. Even after Pru had patiently and matter-of-factly explained about sex and all that, and removed some of the friends more horrendous errors from her mind, it was quite some time before she ceased to find the whole idea of marriage just too bizarre to contemplate when applied to her father and Pru.

* * *

But as adolescence brings entry into the adult world, it also brings a period of narcissist interest in one's own little sphere of life, and in a lesser sense, those who orbit around it. Perhaps she was a late developer in that area, because she was certainly past fifteen before she began to think deeply about who she was, and the why and how of her parentage, and even that only happened by chance, and *via* a wholly innocent spot of eaves-dropping on her part.

When she thought about it at all, she realised she must have been very young when she was told her real father had died before she was born, because she couldn't remember a time when she *didn't* know, but had never actually questioned who he might have been, or how he and her mother had met. Later, after the accident that robbed her of both mother and brother, she had perhaps subconsciously avoided looking too closely into the circumstances of her birth, let alone how it had come about. It was enough that she had the father she'd known

11

all her life, whom she loved and who loved her in return. It took an overheard snippet of conversation between Mrs Buckley and Pru to bring a real curiosity about her parentage leaping to the forefront of Sophie's mind.

* * *

Hawksley Manor, 1961

It was an afternoon in late July, when the heat of the day lay like a soft wool blanket over the countryside, when Red Admiral and Painted Lady butterflies rose and fell lazily above buddleia bushes while bees and other buzzing things fussed over the flower beds. Sophie sat on the warm grass beneath the balustrade of the rear terrace, her back against the wall, reading a slim volume found in the small town library: an essay on the life of Wilfred Owen, written by an American professor, one Ryan L. Petersen. She wanted to read History and English Literature when she went to university next year and the First World War poets fascinated her: they were all so young, and good looking, and romantic…

Deep in her book, she didn't at first hear the approaching footsteps on the paved terrace above her, until they stopped only a few feet away and she heard a long sigh.

'A day like this do remind me of the one the missus and young Rupert died.'

It was Mrs Buckley's voice. Sophie put a finger to keep her place on the page as Mrs Buckley paused then sighed again. 'Miss Sophie was sat on that wall there, waiting for them, and I was over by that tree, setting out the tea things, when the police came…it was almost as bad as the day that chaplain came up from the airfield to tell Mrs de Lacy the captain – well, major he was by then – had been killed…I thought that had to be the worst thing could ever happen in this house; but it wasn't. Not by a long chalk.'

Sophie sat still as a mouse and held her breath.

'Mr Geoffrey did just touch on the matter when I first came, because of Sophie,' Now it was Pru's voice, her tone gently disapproving, 'but I never knew the details, so perhaps you shouldn't be telling them to me now.'

'What can it matter, after all this time,' Mrs Buckley was not to be deflected. 'They were so much in love and he was so handsome and such a gentleman. He crashed over France, they said, just a few days before the master was on his way home from the hospital in North Africa. It fair broke Missis Claire's heart…well we all thought

12

she'd go out of her mind.' She lowered her voice. 'See, her and Mr Geoffrey's marriage hadn't been a good one; not from the start; she was so young and Mr Geoffrey much older and a bit of a lad for the ladies; if you get my meaning. So when the captain came along…well, she fell for him, and he was that crazy for her…Elias used to say he'd never seen a man make love with his eyes as that one did.'

Pru said, 'But Claire and Geoffrey remained together, didn't they, so there must have been something worth salvaging in their relationship.'

'Yes, I think it all came right in the end.' The two began walking again. 'It took time, but strange at it seems, when Miss Sophie was born he was that besotted with her that you'd have thought she really was his own. I always thought that little lass was the start of them staying together and making it work…'

The rest was lost as the pair rounded the corner of the terrace and their voices faded.

Sophie sat transfixed. Sweat gathered along her hairline and slid down her face and she brushed it away with her arm. So, her real father had been in the air force – but where was the airfield the chaplain had come from to tell her mother he was dead? There were old wartime airfields scattered all throughout Hampshire, so it could have been any one of those…

Suddenly, she remembered a warm spring day when she and Rupert had cycled through Belstead wood. They had ridden it seemed for ages, but then she had only been six or thereabouts and her cycle half the size of Rupert's big new Raleigh. He hadn't really wanted her with him, saying it was too far and she would get tired, but she had stubbornly tagged along. The airfield when they reached it she'd found disappointing; quite deserted with most of the Nissan huts rusting, their windows smashed and doors broken. But the brick built control tower remained intact, square and squat and rather ugly; a tattered windsock snapped fitfully in the breeze as they climbed the steps to the railed balcony.

Rupert had been very quiet, so quiet and still that she hadn't liked to ask why they were there, or what he was thinking as he gazed toward the forest and the line of tall trees at the end of the long runway.

Now she realised his thoughts would have been on his Captain Pop, who must have flown from there in the war that everyone, except her father, still talked about as though it had happened only yesterday.

In one of those strange shifts of time and place that sometimes accompany shock she was transported to Rupert's room again, staring down at his album; at the photograph of a tall man in American uniform, with a pair of silver wings on his tunic...

Captain Pop.

She came back to the present with a breathless start. Was it possible? Could Rupert's Captain Pop be her father? But surely, she reasoned, nobody could be called just that: it had to be some kind of childish nickname Rupert had given the man who had been his hero; the man who had fired his determination to join the air force and be a pilot.

So who *was* he, this mystery man her mother had loved so much? She would never know for sure, because she'd die rather than ever, *ever* ask her father, and would never go behind his back and ask Mrs Buckley or Tom or Eli, or anyone else who may have been around at that time...

So she sat on, that late summer's afternoon, her back against the warm stone wall, the American Professor's book in her lap, and wept a few tears at having had the truth almost within her grasp; then dried her eyes and gave herself a good talking to, because all the tears in the world would make no difference: she would never know for certain if she was indeed the daughter of her brother's handsome, and dead, Captain Pop.

Resting her head back against the warm stone wall she sighed. Perhaps she would one day take the path through Belstead wood and see if she could find that old airfield again. But then, she thought drearily, what would be the use; it was all so long ago and there would be little left now to see and no one to ask about the tall American, who had once made love to her mother with his eyes...

CHAPTER 2

Oxford, September 1963

Sophie de Lacy and Ben Nicholls first met in Oxford, at a party in Jeremy Bennett's lodgings on the Banbury Road; a party Sophie thought was in honour of someone's birthday, but an hour into the affair had still not managed to work out who the lucky man, or woman, was.

The basement room was very crowded and hot and she'd got to the stage where she was ready to make an exit; partly because she was bored, and partly because she didn't want to stay until the end and risk being trapped by Jeremy after everyone else had gone. She knew by his unsubtle approach over the past few weeks that he wanted to sleep with her, and she wasn't about to oblige; tonight, or any night. He wasn't her type.

But as she cautiously circled the room in a hopefully not-all-that-obvious progression towards the door and a swift retreat up the basement steps, she became aware of a young man who appeared to be circling the room from the opposite direction, possibly with the same intention to escape. They met by the door; he pushed it open, and with a lift of one eyebrow and an almost imperceptible movement of his head, indicated she should go first. She did, he followed, and they both bolted up the area steps.

He stopped on the pavement. 'Escape from Colditz,' he said, and held out his hand, 'Ben Nicholls.'

Sophie shook hands. 'Sophie de Lacy,' she said primly, and they both burst into a fit of very childish giggles at the ridiculous formality.

'Awful party', he said. 'My brother couldn't come, so he sent me…I think the birthday girl was the daughter of one of his clients. I've probably lost him some business, because I never even got to speak to her.'

'At least you knew who the party was for, I just came along because Jerry invited me, and for once I'd nothing better to do with my evening.'

'There's rash,' he said, and gave her an easy grin. 'I don't know about you, but I'm starving…one cheese sandwich and a glass of cheap plonk does not a supper make: how about a meal at The Mitre?'

The Mitre was well beyond Sophie's means, or those of most of her fellow students, and for a moment she pulled back and took a good look at her companion.

On closer inspection he seemed altogether too tidy, and unless he was a late post-grad, too old to be a student. In general, and in this year of grace, nineteen sixty-three, Oxford students, particularly male ones, were not noted for their sartorial elegance. Long hair, scruffy jeans, cheesecloth shirts and baggy knee-length sweaters were more the style, not the checked Tattersall shirt, tan slacks and double vented tweed sports jacket as worn by Mr Ben Nicholls. With his wavy dark hair cut neatly above his ears, wide brown eyes and the kind of nice, puckish face that would still look much the same into late middle age, he had the appearance of a young businessman relaxing after a day at the office and looking forward to an enjoyable, possibly even randy, evening. This invitation, Sophie decided, had all the signs of a pick-up.

She sighed. 'Look' she said, 'before we get to the wining and dining; how come you left the party in such a hurry, and at the same time as I did?'

'I'm not trying to pick you up,' he said reproachfully, and she blushed. 'I just spotted your crafty bid for freedom and thought I'd do the same…and like I said: I really was there because of my brother.'

'But you're not a student, are you?' It all sounded very plausible, but she still wasn't entirely convinced.

'No, and when I was, it was at Bristol, not Oxford. ' He gave his easy, disarming grin again. 'Now, I really am very hungry – probably almost as hungry as you – I'll bet you didn't eat more than one of those awful sandwiches either; so, how about that dinner?'

He did seem rather nice, and harmless, and fun, and she was ragingly hungry. 'I didn't even eat one,' she said, and he took her arm in a comradely manner.

'Okay. The Mitre it is.'

An obsequious *Maître d'* greeted her companion by name, at the same time managing to give Sophie a quick onceover, as though checking if she were a *bona fide* lady, or a floozy to be sneered at. As she had on her perfectly respectable, knee-high, raw silk shift dress and gave him a haughty look, she apparently passed muster, but as they were ushered to a table she couldn't help wondering if her companion would have been so quick with his invitation to this particular hotel if she'd worn her usual jeans and sweater.

They had a very nice dinner, and Ben didn't make a single pass. They talked all through the meal and by the time they were half-way through the first course he knew she was nineteen, was an only child, had a father but no mother and was in her first year at Summerville reading English Literature and History; home was an old manor house in a small Hampshire village and she hadn't a clue what to do after Oxford. She told him how hard it had been to keep the Manor from being sold; the continuing struggle to maintain it by opening the house and grounds all summer to coach loads of tourists.

'From April through to October is a nightmare,' she said, 'that's when Pru, our housekeeper, and my father retreat to Stable Cottage where Elias used to live. The boys still work the farm, but after they married and started families of their own they moved to new bungalows in the village. Between the farm and the week-end visitors, dad just about manages to keep the whole thing together, but it's a real struggle, and there's never any money left over for any kind of luxuries...'

In return Sophie discovered that Ben was twenty-four; his family home was in Kidlington; his mother's family originated in Provence, where they had settled as Jewish refugees in the late nineteenth century; that Sarah Nicholls was very beautiful and her sprightly and slyly mischievous elderly father, Julius, lived with them; Ben's own father, Hugh, whom he described as rather reserved, but with a dry sense of humour, was a wine importer, and Ben and his older brother, Guy – "a bit of a stick-in-the-mud", both worked in the company offices in Oxford.

'Which is a tad boring and not something I want to do for the rest of my life,' he confided, twirling spaghetti expertly around his fork. 'Working for one's father, and with one's brother, gets a bit incestuous from time to time.'

Sophie had plumped for a crab salad; she wasn't about to risk an errant worm of spaghetti drenched in bolognaise glissading down her best dress, which was an absolute pig to wash and iron.

She asked, 'What would you rather do?'

'I'd like to own a vineyard one day, but that will have to wait awhile. I guess I'll have to go on working in the family firm for now.'

Sophie was amused at his expert thumbnail sketches of his family, wishing secretly that she could talk so freely about her own. His family sounded both exotic and glamorous, making hers seemed dull in comparison. *I've had a much too conventional and sheltered life so far,* she thought, but she sympathised with his feeling of being trapped in a life he didn't really enjoy. There were times when she felt that way herself. Even at Hawksley life could feel a little dull and

17

restricted, and although she loved attending lectures and found university life in general new and exciting, living in the all-women environment of college wasn't at all to her taste.

Ben walked her back to Sommerville, lingering for a few moments by the studded oak door, still opened on the entrance arch. 'Another ten minutes,' she said, 'that door would have been shut and you'd have had to give me a leg-up over the wall.'

He leaned briefly to kiss her lips. 'I'd really like to see you again, Sophie de Lacy.'

'And I'd really like to see you again,' she said.

'When?'

'Saturday night?'

'Sounds good; put on your dancing shoes,' he said.

And that was how it started. Within a month Sophie de Lacy and Ben Nicholls had become an acknowledged pair. He shared a flat with his brother on the outskirts of Oxford on the Woodstock Road, less than a mile from her college, and as Guy had recently become engaged to a fledgling lawyer in Banbury and was seldom in residence at the weekends, they began to spend a good deal of time there, and very soon became lovers: a first for Sophie, although Ben admitted to a couple of short lived affairs since university.

They were blissfully happy: Ben surprised and delighted by Sophie's swift transformation from enjoyable companion to enthusiastic lover, and Sophie amazed at how long it had taken her to realise sex could be such fun. By the approach of the Christmas vacation they knew they were in love, and for the first time in Sophie's life a return home to far off Hawksley had lost something of its charm.

CHAPTER 3

Oxford, November 1963

Drowsy and relaxed, she lay in Ben's warm embrace. Outside it was bone-chillingly cold, and the prospect of leaving the warm cocoon of bed to brave the icy wind at present whipping down the Woodstock Road, was becoming less attractive by the minute. It would be better, Sophie thought, if she could live away from the college, which even now still had rules and regulations irksome to many of its under-graduates. If she had her own place, however small, they could spend whole days and nights together, instead of just a few snatched hours before she had to return to college.

'Only another hour and we'll have to make a move,' Ben interrupted her thoughts, then, as if denying his words, groaned and wrapped his arms more closely around her. 'Oh, Sophie, darling, I do love you so much…lord, but I wish you could stay the whole night.'

She laughed, 'Are you thought-reading now? I want to move out of Hall next year and wondering if I could have my own place rather than share some grotty digs with another undergrad. Mind you,' she was suddenly thoughtful, 'I don't know how my father would view it but it would probably be less expensive than college so that might persuade him it was a good idea.'

Ben rubbed his head against hers, 'Tell me about your dad – I don't really know much about him and I like to have some idea what I'll be up against when I ask for your hand in marriage!'

She teased, 'You have to ask *me* first.'

'I will,' he said, '*after* you've told me everything – about you and your dad and Hawksley; what happened to your mother and all that.'

She said obliquely, 'If I do you might just change your mind about asking me.'

He ruffled her hair, 'Oh, get on with it, will you…'

Once again she fell silent; for so long this time that he had to bite back the urge to tell her again to get on with it, but he was a patient man and willing to wait. At last she gave a sigh. 'I'd better start at the beginning…tell you about the day dad and mother had gone to fetch Rupert from school…'

Ben settled his arms about her. 'You don't have to if it hurts,' he said, 'I'd never want you to do that, Sophie darling.'

She turned her head and looked into his eyes. 'I've never really talked about it – ever – but I'd like, I *want* to tell you. So this is how it was…

'It was a lovely sunny July afternoon and I was nine years old. I'd had chicken pox and was still at the scabby stage so I hadn't gone with my parents when they went to collect Rupert. I remember I was sitting on the balustrade of the rear terrace, feeling cross because they were late – later than they'd ever been before and if they didn't come soon I'd have hardly any time with Rupert before I had to go to bed: I wouldn't even be able to hug him in case I gave *him* the chicken pox, in the way my best friend Victoria had given it to me.

'Mrs Buckley was fussing around the table set up under the chestnut tree: putting damp napkins over the sandwiches to stop them from curling and setting the muslin cover over the fruit cake she'd baked that morning especially for Rupert's return. I'd picked a bunch of wild flowers from the big meadow to go on his bedroom windowsill and I remember I wished I'd picked some more to put on the table.

'It was Gunner, Rupert's old Labrador, who heard the car first. I saw him get up from beneath the tea table and began to trot around the side of the house. Mrs Buckley called, "I think they're here, Miss Sophie," and as I jumped down she added, "now remember, don't go too close to your brother, he won't want to spend half his summer holiday with spots all over him…"'

Sophie paused; gave a twisted little smile. 'Funny how those first few minutes are still so clear in my mind: how people looked, what they did, everything that was said. It was only later it all became confused and disjointed…I remember running through the open French windows to the front of the house; my grandma was standing at the open front door and as I ran towards her she half-turned, gesturing me to stay back, but I'd waited long enough: I shouted, "Roop, Roop, R*oo*pert!" and ran past her and out onto the steps.'

Sophie paused again and Ben felt her catch her breath a moment, but she went on, her voice steady. 'There was a strange car in the drive; the car Gunner heard wasn't the old Land Rover but a black car with a blue light on the roof. I watched as a uniformed policeman and policewoman climbed from it and start up the steps. The policeman took of his cap, he said very quietly to my grandmother, "I am Superintendent Marshall from Beaulieu, Madam. I need to speak with you at once," he looked at me then and said: "perhaps someone could take the little girl to another part of the house."

'By now Mrs Buckley had arrived, she said, "Come along, Miss

Sophie, you can help me make the Superintendent and the young lady a pot of tea while they talk to Madam."

'I didn't want to go, but she had a firm grip on my hand so I did as I was told. I was trying to puzzle what they could want, and why they had to come now, just when Rupert would be arriving at absolutely any minute. I hoped they wouldn't stay long and expect tea...I remember saying: "We shan't give them any fruit cake shall we, Bucky dear? We have to keep *that* for Rupert."'

Sophie gave a little hiccup of laughter that ended in a sob. 'It was one hell of a long time before I thought about the fruit cake again, and wondered what had happened to it, and the sandwiches, and the freshly made lemonade that had been keeping cool in the larder. Almost a year passed before I'd finally accept that my mother and Rupert would never be coming home at all; that their return had only been as far as Hawksley churchyard.'

Ben felt her struggle to hold back her tears; but knew she needed to say more. How on earth had she kept it all bottled up for so long?He stroked her hair gently. 'Tell me how it happened.'

She gave along shudder. 'A container lorry crashed into the side of the Land Rover; it killed my mother and Rupert outright and crippled my father for life. My grandmother was devastated and died quite soon after; I suppose she never recovered from the shock and I was in such a confused state I scarcely even registered her death. I was still waiting, believing that in some miraculous way my mother and Rupert would come home again. It was months later, just before my tenth birthday that dad came home from the hospital, with a strange woman in a nurse's grey uniform pushing him in a wheelchair.

'It think it was then I knew and understood for the first time that they were never coming home, and my father was the one thing left to me of my past life.'

She paused then for so long that he wondered if she was finished, but something about the restless little movement of her head against his arm kept him silent; shrewdly diving that there was more to come.

'Well, you'll have to know, sooner or later, I suppose' when she spoke again it was almost briskly. 'Fact is, Geoffrey isn't my real father – *he* was killed in the war before I was born, but nobody talks about that...I imagine my mother told me when I was very young, because it's something I've always known, but since she died nobody, including Dad, has ever mentioned it and I suppose I was too happy with the father I had to want to rock the boat by asking him about the

21

one I never knew.'

Ben was startled; he propped on one elbow and looked at her in disbelief. 'But – how could you *not* want to know about him?'

She said stonily, 'Well, he was dead, so there wasn't much point, was there? Anyway, by the time I was eight, me and my friend Joyce had figured out that as Rupert *was* Geoffrey's son and nine years older than me, my mother must have had a wartime affair of which I was the result.' Her voice softened and again she gave a small, twisted smile. 'At that time it all seemed terribly romantic to be some unknown soldier's love child. Later, when I'd worked out that if Geoffrey came home in the March of the year I was born in the December, it made his return pretty close to my real father's death, so there was a good chance either might have fathered me: certainly Geoffrey's name is on my birth certificate. It might only have been as I grew older and still looked nothing like any other member of the family, past or present, that it became obvious I wasn't a genuine de Lacy.'

'And you *still* don't know who your real father was – or want to?' asked Ben, and saw her gaze shift fractionally from his. 'You whopping fibber,' he breathed, 'you do know, don't you?'

She sighed. 'Not really, not absolutely...see, there is this photo album of Rupert's I found years ago when I was just a kid. There were loads of pictures of a man – an American pilot. At the time I thought he looked familiar and I overheard some gossip a few years later that really set me thinking, but there was nothing to *prove* he was my father. It wasn't until the evening before I left for Oxford, when I was in my room with my hair tied back trying out some new make-up in front of the mirror, I suddenly realised *why* he looked familiar.' She grinned and spread her hands. 'I should have twigged ages before, because we have the same shaped face and he was really blonde like me, although I don't know what colour his eyes were; they could have been any colour because I only have black and white pictures of him.'

Ben was nonplussed. 'Well, bugger me,' he said.

She looked at him, suddenly solemn. 'Now you know the awful truth: that I am a woman subject to a bar sinister, with not one, but two, fathers,' she said, 'are you sure you still want to pop the question?'

Ben pulled her into his arms again. 'Marry me, darling Sophie, and you can have my dad as well.

* * *

22

On her return home, but for the constant ache of her separation from Ben, Sophie slipped easily back into her accustomed niche in the household, but within less than forty-eight hours she had become aware that this time something was different.On the surface the house was the same: Pru and her father their usual welcoming selves, and yet beneath the apparently calm and unruffled surface of life at the manor there ran a subtle but unmistakable undercurrent; even dear, dependable Bucky appeared to have a faintly distracted air about her, while Eli and Tom looked positively furtive the first time Sophie clapped eyes on them.

'What's the matter with you two?' she demanded, when at the end of her second day at Hawksley, she'd managed to run the pair to earth where they were eating their lunch in the tractor shed. 'You've been avoiding me ever since I came home.'

'Haven't,' they both said in unison. It was quite funny to see two grown men look shifty and she almost took pity on them.

'Look,' she said, 'are we pals or not?' They both nodded in a kind of hapless fashion. 'Well, then, all pals together, tell me why I've the feeling everyone here is hiding some big secret.'

'It's yon two up at t'house,' Eli offered reluctantly.

'What two?'

Tom snorted. 'Them two, o'course: your dad an' Pru.'

'What about them?' Sophie plumped down on a hay bale and took one of Eli's sandwiches.

'They'm sweet on each other, that's what.' Tom made a smacking sound with his lips. 'Holding hands, gettin' all lovey-dovy an' hiding away in Stable cottage when visitors is about.'

Sophie almost choked on her mouthful of cheese and pickle. Eli thumped her on the back. 'Steady lass, Tom's crude, like, but he's right. Real close they'm become ...'specially since you been away so much this last year. They must guess old Buckley an' us ul' know be now: reckon whole folk in village will soon an' all if they'm don't already.' He took a swig of tea and belched. 'So I daresay they'd be telling you soon enough.' Sophie began to laugh, remembering her own long ago fantasy of being a bridesmaid at Pru and her father's wedding. Just how long *had* they been "sweet on each other", she wondered, but been smart enough to keep it all under wraps.

'How simply marvellous,' she spluttered. 'Oh, but won't it be just great watching them trying to find the right moment to tell me!'

'Aar,' said Eli with a huge grin, 'reckon it will an' all.'

But of course, being Sophie, she couldn't wait and came down to breakfast the following morning with a breezy: 'So, when's the wedding going to be?' then burst out laughing as her father almost choked on his tea and Pru dropped the skillet she was about to place on the range, frightening Boris the cat, who spat and leaped from his place on the dresser.

As Pru rescued the skillet Sophie took a piece of her father's toast and spread marmalade generously. 'Funny thing, but years ago I fantasised about the two of you getting married so I could be a bridesmaid. At this late stage I hope you're not expecting me to float down the aisle after you wearing a pink frilly dress.'

'God forbid,' Geoffrey growled. 'It will be a very quiet affair: definitely no bridesmaids.'

Sophie took a bite out of her toast and chewed thoughtfully for a moment before saying casually, 'If you hang around a bit, we could make it a double.'

'It would have been nice,' she told Ben that night on the telephone, 'to have a picture of their two faces as a keepsake!'

'Tell me,' he begged, 'what happened when you told him about us – did he say: "wash your mouth out?"'

'Not quite,' she gave a gurgle of laughter, 'but he did do the: "You-are-much-too-young-to-even-be-thinking-about-marriage-yet" thing. I almost said: "and you are much too old," but managed to keep my mouth shut. Even so, it still got a bit heated and hairy for a while.'

'We're going to have to wait forever, aren't we?' Ben tried not to sound as despondent as he felt; after all, it was only what they'd both expected.

'Maybe not that long, but certainly until I've got my degree and hit the magic twenty-one; but he has agreed to me having my own place next year. He and Pru will come to Oxford after Christmas and help me find digs or a small flat to rent.' She paused a moment, then added: 'They want to meet you at the same time, so be sure you clean up nice and mind your P's & Q's, lover.'

'Oh, God,' he groaned and Sophie could almost hear the sweat break out on his brow. 'I suppose I'd better tell my folks as well before then...Oh bloody hell, Soph; suppose they want to do the 'let's get together and meet the in-laws' thing?'

She gave a shriek of laughter. 'Oh, they will, they will – and that could mean pistol's at dawn!' she said.

In the event, the meetings, first between Ben and her parents at

Hawksley, followed in the New Year by a meeting with the Nicholls family at their home in Kidlington, had been amiable and relaxed and gone without a hitch, both sides. Only the octogenarian Julius, who had mischievously voted for an immediate wedding to 'save the young people's sanity,' had agreed that they should wait until the December of the following year, when Sophie would have both finished her degree and reached her twenty first birthday.

That first hurdle taken, Ben had become a regular weekend visitor at Hawksley, where he was captivated by the old house and quickly became at ease with Pru and Geoffrey. Sophie in her turn was charmed with Ben's parents, and although a little wary of his very conventional older brother, had fallen absolutely head over heels in love with Julius, who was known to one and all as papa. His humour, his wisdom and above all his humanity, drew her to him and she could understand why Ben was closer to his grandfather than perhaps he was to his own parents.

CHAPTER 4

Oxford, May 1965

At first it all seemed so simple: they were in love, they would get married and then spend the rest of their lives together. And that was how it had been in the beginning, apart from her initial shock and dismay when Geoffrey told her gently that he had decided when she married Ben the manor would be theirs, to do with as they wished. It was now far too big and difficult for Pru to manage, he said, adding with a wry smile that neither of them was getting any younger and it was one hell of a distance for him to get from one room to another on his crutches. Stable Cottage was large enough for comfort and small enough for Pru to run single handed, with someone to help out occasionally with the housework.

Once over the shock Sophie had to acknowledge that he was right; she knew from experience that there were times when it took a huge effort of will for her father even to get on his feet and it was a constant nagging worry for Pru on the occasions she had to leave him with only Mrs Buckley to keep an eye on him. The housekeeper, although still only in her mid-forties, would struggle to get Geoffrey back on his feet should he fall.

He was always so impatient, so fiercely independent, that by noon, when weariness and pain inevitably forced him into his wheelchair for the remainder of the day, it was as though all life was suddenly drained from his body. Those mornings when the pain was particularly bad and he had to rely solely on the chair, he was like the proverbial bear with a sore head.

Ben had been equally shocked and even more dismayed when Sophie told him her father's decision. 'My God,' he'd commented, 'don't leave me alone for a minute in that place – I may never find you again – and what about my job? All may have been lovey-dovey at the Great Parental Get-Together but Pa will hit the ceiling when he hears I'll have to leave the firm and move to Hampshire.'

'Well, you've said more than once that you want out,' commented Sophie, 'so here's your chance!

'I know moving to Hampshire is perfect for both of us,' said Ben, 'and I'm a lucky guy – I don't know of any other types who get a gorgeous girl *and* a country seat all in one go! But I still need to earn a living – and what on earth are we to do with the place? It's huge and there are acres of grounds; the farm and everything... You said your father struggles to keep the place from falling down. We could never afford to maintain the house *and* run an estate like that: anything I might earn would be a drop in the ocean.'

Sophie propped her chin on one hand and gazed into space. It was a glorious spring day and they were seated on the river bank a mile or so out of the town, the remains of a picnic on the grass between them. Eventually she said, 'Of course, the East and West wing haven't been lived in for years, not really since some Ministry took them over during the war; now nobody goes into them except for the visitors when the whole house is opened up through the summer. It isn't all that big – not by some standards but maybe we could do something better with it than limp along as we do at present just trying to attract the tourists.'

'Such as?'

'Oh, I don't know...turn it into a Conference Centre...there's a lot of that going on at the moment; or like Kenwood, as a venue for concerts and plays.' She giggled, 'How about "A Season of the Bard at Hawksley Manor..."'

'Too far off the beaten track for the first and would initially cost too much; you'd need hordes of staff to cook and clean and serve meals...and the same goes for your second bright idea,' interrupted Ben.

'Yes, you're right.' She was suddenly despondent.

'On the other hand...' Ben was thoughtful and his eyes took on a far-away look. 'The soil, what I've seen of it, is very good, and you could do a lot more with that whacking great meadow at the side of the house than use it to graze sheep and cut for hay...it must be a good four acres at least.'

She said idly, 'And what would *you* do with it?'

'Do?' he grinned. 'Me? I'd plant a vineyard,' he said.

Sophie was incredulous, 'A vineyard – in *England*?'

'There are more than one of those here already and turning out some interesting wines,' he countered.

'Oh yes? And how much would *that* cost?' she asked.

'I don't know,' he said, 'but if it's possible I'd love to do it.'

Sophie thought hard for a moment. 'Mad, you're mad!' she said then laughed suddenly and turned to fling her arms around his neck. 'So let's do it!' she said.

Ben caught her to him. 'Yeah, let's do it...just you and me together, Soph; imagine: *'The Hawksley Manor Sauvignon!'* He gave a shout of laughter and they rolled together over the short, springy turf. After a few breathless moments they sat up, grinning broadly at each other. 'Tell you what,' said Ben, 'now you have the lovely Pru's little Mini on more or less permanent loan, we'll drive over to Kidlington the next weekend we're both free and ask Papa Julius what he thinks.'

Sophie was doubtful. 'But he was a wine *merchant* and you told me he's been out of the business for years. He's old and probably won't want to be bothered.'

Ben said patiently, 'Sophie, darling, there's one hell of a lot of my family history you don't yet know...papa Julius was a wine *grower* in Germany for over thirty years; fortunately he was quick to see the way the wind was blowing and came to England well before Hitler came to power. For eight years he worked as a book keeper to a firm of wine importers in London and saved every penny he earned until he'd enough money to begin his own import business.' He gave a crow of laughter. 'Sophie, my grandfather cared a great deal more about growing his own wine than he ever did in selling other peoples.'

Sophie cupped her chin in one hand and gazed at him solemnly. 'So all we need to do,' she said, 'is find some way of making enough money to prepare the ground and buy the vines and plant and nurture them for...how many years before they produce a harvest?'

'Um, about three or four?' he said tentatively.

'Oh, great,' she said, 'I was beginning to think it might be difficult!'

* * *

For a week or more they talked over the venture; enthusiastic and up in the clouds one moment; doubtful and down to earth the next. Sophie dreamed her way through lectures and Ben drew doodles at his office desk and drove his father mad with his inattention to the business of selling wine. Eventually, worn out with fruitless speculation they agreed the whole subject of vineyards should be taboo until they could lay the idea before his grandfather, which they did at the first opportunity.

* * *

Julius Berger settled back in his creaking old leather armchair and took an appreciative mouthful of wine. 'Ah,' he held the glass to the light, 'a very nice gift for an old man…the very best: I think from a little vineyard in a valley a few kilometres south of Tours…could it be from Dominic?' He chuckled. 'You see, my Benyamin, although the taste buds, they are not as they used to be, I can still tell a fine wine and its provenance.'

Sophie laughed and Ben said: 'If I didn't know better, I'd think you'd read the label.' He stretched out in his own chair. 'I wouldn't mind having a week or two in France with Dominic this summer, but Dad's hinting I should tour some of the Bulgarian vineyards – I think he wants to get his money's worth out of me before I move to Hampshire.' He shook his head in disgust. 'Last week I tried a Bulgarian red; talk about rough stuff,' he shuddered. 'I'd rather drink drain cleaner!'

'All in a day's work,' Julius gave his foxy grin. 'Now, what has brought you two young people to see an old man on this fine afternoon? – not to talk about Bulgarian wine, I am sure.'

'We've come for your advice, papa.' As usual, Ben came straight to the point. 'When Sophie and I are married and take over the manor, we just have to find some way to make it pay its way.'

Sophie leaned forward to put a hand on the old man's arm. 'Ben has a wonderful idea of how we might help do that, but we need you to tell us if it's possible, or just a pipe dream.'

'Then let me hear it, my dears.'

Ben took a deep breath. 'The Manor is beautiful and certainly historic enough to attract plenty of visitors. It isn't a grand palace: more a Tudor gentleman's country residence, but it does come with a lot of land, most of it put down to cereal crops, but there's one spot in particular…a meadow close to the house and probably as much as four acres: south facing, well drained and because it's been grazed alternate years and left fallow in between, it's good, fertile topsoil over a deep bed of chalk. Sophie and I have talked this over, papa; *I* think the land is perfect for a small vineyard … I'm prepared to work as hard and as long as needed to make a go of it, but I need advice, lots of it.' He gave a little, lop-sided grin. 'I know plenty about buying and selling wine, but not much about producing it.'

'Hmm.' Julius stroked his chin. 'I take it you would just want to grow the grapes and contract a winery to process and bottle the harvest?'

Ben nodded, 'Of course; to actually make the wine would not only cost more than we could ever raise for all the equipment we would need, we'd also have to employ quite a few staff and we really do want to do manage and run this ourselves with as little extra help as possible, at least until it's properly established.'

Julius raised his eyebrows. 'And when we talk of money: the vines, they will not come cheap. What do you have to spend?'

'Not much,' Ben admitted ruefully, 'I still have my share of the eighteen hundred pounds Uncle Boris left between Guy and me; Sophie's father has contracted a very generous annual amount towards the upkeep of the manor for the first five years, but we feel we have to keep that in hand for any unexpected setbacks, rather than spend it as it comes.'

Julius nodded approval, 'Quite right, my dears.'

'Our first idea was to both get jobs and save hard for a couple of years,' Ben continued, 'so that we might be able to fund perhaps a couple of acres of vines to begin with. That sounded all right until we really thought it through.'

'The trouble is that most of the actual physical work for any vineyard will fall on Ben's shoulders,' Sophie put in. 'You see, although I can help with the business side of any venture, I shall be needed at the Manor full time, just to keep it ticking over. Pru is no spring chicken now and needs to retire along with dad...even when they are married she will still be his full time nurse as well as mistress of Keepers Cottage.'

'So what will be your duties...which will be, I suppose, all for love?'

Sophie made a face. 'It certainly won't be for money. I shall help Ben keep the books for the vineyard, organise and oversee the cleaning staff and take over as many of the house tours as possible, instead of paying the two professional guides to do all that as dad has in the past – and that's just for starters. When Ben and I are settled at Hawksley we inherit *all* the responsibilities that go with it: the Home Farm, the worker's wages, renting the fields out for grazing, pollarding the woodland, the winter logging...the list is endless.'

'This is much responsibility for you, my child.'

Sophie answered quietly, 'I was born to it, and I can do it; because the only alternative is to sell the house...*if* we could find a buyer in today's market. But my father is getting on, papa. He's been badly disabled for many years and his health has been slowly deteriorating all that time. He's fought a long hard battle to keep Hawksley and I don't want to be the one to break his heart by having to let it go in his lifetime.'

Julius tilted his head back and was silent for perhaps a minute. Eventually he lowered his head again and bent his keen old eyes on Sophie. 'Then I think that together we three must find a solution.' He smiled; such a loving, gentle smile that Sophie was suddenly close to tears. 'So, Mistress Sophie, I think I must come soon and see this so old and loved house and this perhaps someday-to-be vineyard...then we shall see, my dears.' He nodded his head and repeated: 'we shall see...but for now... Benyamin, if you will...another glass of Dominic's wine, ja?

* * *

Ben, his grandfather and Sophie motored down to Hampshire together the following weekend; Ben driving them in his grandfather's old Lagonda, Julius refusing to trust himself to Pru's bright yellow mini. "Julius does not ride in such a carriage," he said, politely but firmly, so they travelled instead in great comfort and style.

Secretly Sophie was relieved; since moving from college into her much longed-for private space – a small basement sitting room with an even smaller bedroom, minuscule kitchen and bathroom in Cranham Street – the mini had proved a blessing for weekend trips to Kidlington or Hawksley, but would have fallen far short of a luxurious ride for Julius' ancient bones.

The open house was in full swing when they arrived at the manor, with two coaches and numerous cars in the recently extended gravelled car park at the side of the house. Ben stopped before the front entrance steps and when he and Sophie had helped his grandfather from the car, stood in silence for a few moments, one either side of the old man, as he gazed up at the imposing doorway. Sophie pressed his arm gently and said, 'Welcome to Hawksley Papa Julius. What would you like to see first?'

'Oh, I think perhaps this meadow in which my grandson wishes to plant his vines.'

They made their way around to the back of the house, via the balustrade terrace, the wild thyme that grew between the flagstones releasing a heady fragrance beneath their footsteps, and descended the broad stone steps down into the formal gardens, the trim box-hedged beds filled with tightly budded roses. With Julius leaning on Ben's arm they passed through the opening in the eight foot high yew hedge and walked slowly around the walled fruit and vegetable garden to where the lake lay almost motionless, just a faint rippling here and there betraying the presence of slender Golden Orff moving just below the surface. Taking the gravel path towards the stables they came at last to the iron courting gate that gave access to the big meadow, on the far side of which stood another gate; an iron one now, in place of the old wooden five-barred affair, and beyond that the broad sandy ride through Belstead wood.

Sophie halted suddenly, feeling an eerie sensation; almost as though time had stopped; a flash of memory holding her immobile as she gazed across the meadow, her hands tight on the rough iron surface of the courting gate...

On the old wooden gate before Belstead wood her mother had sat, her hand on the shoulder of the man standing beside her: the tall, flaxen-haired American pilot who had been Claire de Lacy's lover, and perhaps Sophie's own lost father, his head tilted towards her mother's laughing face; Rupert's Captain Pop, captured on a little boy's camera: frozen in time, all those summers ago...

'Sophie, are you all right?' Ben's concerned voice sent the image flying and she came back into the present; to the warm spring sunshine and her own lover's beloved face. She smiled at him and put her hand up to his cheek.

'I'm fine,' she said and turned to Julius. 'Now papa, what do you think of our meadow?'

'I think it is a long walk from the house for an old man,' he said mildly, 'but I think also perhaps a journey worth my while.' Passing through the gate he walked a few yards into the field, then stooped and dug strong old fingers into the ground, still moist from overnight rain. 'Yes,' he stood upright and gazed down at his fingers smeared with earth. 'You are right, my Benyamin. This is good soil for vines to grow; a slight slope, south facing with good drained pasture and chalk beneath so they must put down strong deep roots to find moisture.' He turned and smiled at them both. 'Now we shall see this house which is much too big for two people and must earn its keep; then we sit and talk,' he said.

* * *

Whenever Sophie looked back on that day she never ceased to marvel that someone as old as Julius, and from such a different time and place, could have so quickly grasped the difficulties she and Ben would face in turning the house and estate from a liability into an asset.

After their tour of the house was complete, they had visited the estate office to see the overall plans of Hawksley; Julius questioning Sophie closely about the Home Farm and land; later, after all three had lunched with Geoffrey and Pru at Keepers Cottage, he relaxed into a comfortable armchair in the snug sitting room.

'There is much hard work to be done and it will take time,' he said, peering over his spectacles. 'Benyamin is right, the vineyard would be good, and should begin to show a profit in perhaps three to four years. He shall have his vineyard but will need a partner with a little money to invest...' he grinned mischievously at Ben, 'albeit a sleeping one, but that is for the future; for now we must think of other things.'

He smiled gently at Geoffrey where he sat in his chair, with Pru perched on the arm. 'You have had, I think a long hard struggle and it is right you should step back and enjoy your time together...Sophie and Ben; they are young and full of energy and ready to let you do that. Now there is much planning to do for this wedding so soon after Christmas...ayeesh!' he gave a gusty sigh, 'my daughter talks of little else these past weeks already; but we also shall steal time to make plans for this vineyard – and for the manor. For these young people, next year will see the start of many things.'

* * *

After that momentous day with Julius at Hawksley the weeks appeared to fly past; Sophie, working on the run up to her finals, used what little spare time she had to make her own plans for their first year together at the Manor, while Ben sat for long hours after work with Julius; planning a trip to France in the New Year, first to ask the advice of his friend, Dominic de la Tour, on the proposed vineyard and to choose and order the first three acres of young vines suitable for their Hampshire soil. Julius would be the 'sleeping partner' and provide the bulk of the money; Ben would be the labourer and provide the muscle.

'Papa writes the cheques and I sweat blood tilling the soil,' commented Ben wryly to Sophie on one of their rare evenings together. 'How's that for a division of labour?'

'What do you mean – sweat blood,' Sophie demanded loftily, 'all the tractors, ploughs, harrows you could wish for are already at the farm waiting for you...not to mention Eli and Tom, who won't be able to resist rolling up their sleeves and joining in. I reckon I've got the mucky end of the stick sorting out the house!' She gave a theatrical sigh and lay back against the pillows, her arms clasped behind her head.

Ben tousled her hair. 'Poor old Soph...I know it was your idea, but are you sure you can cope with opening to the public four days a week all through the season instead of just the weekends?'

'Of course I can. I've worked it all out. We'll open Saturday through to Tuesday from ten to six from April to October, so I'll have three days a week to keep up with all the paper work; Eli's wife is going to share the house tours with me and Tom's wife is getting together a rota of cleaners to do a couple of hours early morning before the hoards arrive.' She paused and gave a sigh of satisfaction. 'The truly perfect part is that now Pete Morgan is eager to rent – and if possible in a year or two – buy the home farm, all the paper work on that will be off my back...and one hell of an expense off the estate in general. The farm has barely made a profit for years now.'

'That offer from Morgan was a big stroke of luck – but it took your father by surprise all right,' said Ben. 'I'm not too sure he actually likes the idea.'

'He doesn't,' Sophie said, 'but he promised he wouldn't interfere in any decisions we may make, and he'll keep his word. Actually, I guessed the change at home farm was in the wind...Eli told me ages ago that Pete's wanted to rent the farm and all the pasture he could get for the past five or six years, but didn't think there was any chance my father would play ball.' She shrugged. 'My dad is of the old school of landowners who hate letting go any part of their estates. But this is the nineteen-sixties and we have to be realists: the farm has always been mainly agricultural with just the odd flock of sheep grazing the big field and the meadows at Barrow's End, so very labour intensive. While the farm is tied to the Manor it's all lumped together for tax purposes, and like every other big landowner since the war, Dad's been whacked for just about every kind of tax the Government can think of....On the other hand, one tenant farmer going it alone, will get oodles of help from the present government to turn it into a modern beef and dairy farm, which is what Pete's itching to do.'

'Well, it's a relief to think there's at least one major problem solved.' Ben rumpled his own hair into a cockscomb. 'But, gosh, Soph, when you've got your degree and gone back to Hawksley, I'm going to miss this place and all the lovely hours we've spent here these last months; soon this part of our lives and all the freedom we've had will be over for ever.'

'But it has been lovely, hasn't it,' she said, 'to have that time; just to laze around and forget for a few hours all the bother of your work and my exams...'

He drew her down into his arms. 'God, Sophie, but I love and need you so much,' he said huskily. 'Once you leave Oxford I think I'll go into a decline like some Victorian heroine.'

She said: 'Well, my lease for this place doesn't run out until October, so we still have until then to make hay,' then added with mock severity, 'I believe you only want me for my body, you cad!'

'Who can blame me; it is rather a nice one.'

He began to walk his fingers down her throat to her shoulder, then to her breast and she gave a desperate little laugh and wrapped her arms around him.

'Have you ever thought,' she said, 'how *I* am going to manage without *you*?'

'All the time,' he murmured as his mouth found hers, 'I think about it all the time; but not right now...'

CHAPTER 5

Hampshire, October 1965

There were times during those last three months before their wedding, when both Ben and Sophie seriously considered eloping to Gretna Green well before the event. It was a wonder, Sophie said, that she had actually managed to obtain a creditable first and second degree.

'I can't wait for it all to be over so that we can pack our bags and get away from everyone and everything for a few weeks,' she moaned piteously. 'If I have to endure one more mention of guest lists and bridesmaids dresses I shall probably throw myself from the top of the church tower...did your mother *have* to produce all those cute little girl cousins to traipse behind me down the aisle? I thought you were Jewish.'

'Ma is, in a very loose, non-orthodox way but my pa's father was a Bishop and the girls are all from his side of the family – hell of a mixture, that.' Ben was apologetic. 'Try and bear with my mother Soph; she really would have liked at least one daughter. Instead she got lumbered with a couple of boys – I have a sneaking suspicion she feels sons are more trouble than they're worth when it comes to weddings; poor dear, she did have to take a back seat and let the mother of the bride do it all when Guy and Geraldine got hitched.'

Sophie straightened her back from the last packing case filled with books and a multitude of oddments acquired over her months for her dear little flat in Cranham Street. 'Very well,' she said, 'to please your mama I'll try and be patient, and I *am* truly grateful she's taken a lot of the tedious stuff off Pru's shoulders. Now...'she looked around the room at the collection of boxes and carrier bags, 'is that everything? Pru and daddy will be here with the Land Rover any time now...I hope all this will fit in the back as the Mini is already full to the roof. I can't *think* how I've managed to collect such a load of stuff in such a short space of time.'

'I can,' said Ben, 'you must have emptied half the book shops and junk stalls in Oxford since you left Hall; did you really need all these books on the war poets for your degree – there must be at least a couple of dozen of the damned things.'

'No, not all; most are just for my own pleasure.'

He sat down on a packing case and pulled her into his arms. 'I wish you could pack me up and take me with you.'

She cupped his face in her hands and very gently kissed his lips. 'So do I, but as your father is getting rid of you to Australia early next month for a whole three weeks, if I bore you off to Hawksley *before* then I'd be in his bad books for ever more.'

Ben laughed. 'He hasn't quite forgiven me yet for deserting the firm, but now Guy's settled and doing all the right things for the business, I think he'll hardly notice I've gone. This trip to Australia is just his way of saying: "make the most of it boy; it's your last chance to be a successful businessman like me and your brother!'

There was a sudden loud raucous toot from the street and they looked at each other ruefully. 'That's an end to our last cuddle session for a while,' Ben said. For a long moment they stayed close in each other's arms until another toot sounded, this time a double one.

Sophie sighed and kissed him again. 'That's my dad, impatient as ever,' she said, and went to open the door.

With the main house now closed to the public until next spring, Sophie expected her father and Pru to be in high spirits at once more reclaiming the manor as their own, but when their two vehicle caravan finally arrived at Hawksley and all her belongings had been unloaded into a spare bedroom, Sophie gradually became aware of a most disturbing of air of tension hovering around the house.

When lunch was over and Geoffrey had retired to his own room for a nap, she and Pru began unpacking and sorting through some of the boxes. They worked in companionable silence for a while until Sophie broke it to ask casually. 'Is everything alright, Pru?'

'So far as I know...' Pru held up a stuffed rabbit. 'Do you really need this?'

'Yes, Ben won it at the summer fair...but you haven't really answered my question.'

'What makes you think anything might not be?' Pru delved deeper into the packing case and held up an enormously long multi-coloured stripped scarf at arm's length. 'Oh, my God,' she said, 'don't tell me you actually wear this thing.'

Exasperated, Sophie snatched it out of her hand. 'I do, and stop messing about or I'll scream...dad's really miffed about something, *you* are looking decidedly shifty and this place fairly reeks of suspense; so what's been going on?'

Pru remained impassive. 'It's nothing much...one of the visitors was hanging around Stable Cottage last week end and you know how your father is when anyone strays off limits. I gather they had a few words and he's been grumpy ever since. Really, Sophie, it's nothing to bother about.'

In a pig's eye, it isn't, Sophie thought; she could shoot peas through that explanation, but when Pru got that guileless look on her face it was a waste of time pushing her. Mrs Buckley would probably be a lot easier than Pru to wheedle any information about the odd atmosphere now hanging over the manor like ectoplasm.

'Oh, I don't really know, my dear...' Mrs Buckley shook her head and gave the dough she was kneading an extra hard thump. 'There was some sort of upset last Sunday...' she paused and dusted more flour over the dough. 'See, Mr Geoffrey and me were in the kitchen having a cup of coffee, when Pru come in looking all pink an' flustered. "Geoffrey," she says, "we have to talk", and off they go's into the pantry and shuts the door so I couldn't hear no more.'

'What happened after that?' Sophie hitched onto the kitchen table. This was better, she thought; trust dear old Bucky to know *something*.

'Well now, Pru she went back to wait for the next tour to arrive and Mr Geoffrey he gets into his wheelchair and I see him go past the window: fair pushing it along he was and he come back about twenty minutes later looking right put out.' She stopped, looking perplexed. 'He was that mazed and upset he couldn't even finish his elevenses ...and you know how your pa is for his morning coffee an' cake.'

'Didn't he say anything at all?'

'Not a word, my dear. Just sat in that chair over there looking all put out until Pru come in at lunch time and they went back down to the cottage. After an hour she goes back to the reception desk and Mr. Geoffrey stayed at the cottage and didn't come back up again 'till the next day.'

'Hum,' Sophie was baffled. Well, whoever the mysterious visitor had been, he certainly seemed to have put the cat amongst the pigeons; it took an awful lot to rattle her father and even more to get Pru in a twist.

She slid off the table and took herself off to the big meadow to think. Leaning on the iron kissing gate she cupped her chin in her hands and gazed broodingly across the meadow towards Belstead Wood.

'Curioser and curioser,' she said out loud, 'but unless either Pru or Pa lets something slip, I'm unlikely to discover just who the phantom visitor was and what he did to get everyone in such a tizzy.'

She wished Ben were there with her to share the mystery. She gave a wry smile. Only a few hours but so many miles apart, and she

was already missing him terribly... *Roll on December*, she thought, *roll on wedding day*, and smiled again, quoting softly:
   '"Christ, that I were in my bed
   And my love in my arms again!"'

* * *

As the weeks passed, Sophie pushed to the back of her mind her unsettling homecoming. Everything appeared to have returned more or less to normal: Pru and her father seemed their old reliable selves, and Sophie herself was too busy shuttling to and from Oxfordshire in her bright yellow Mini to notice that a faint, but persistent tension lingered still beneath all the outward placidity of the household.

While Ben was in Australia she spent every weekend at Kidlington, feeling duty bound to help his mother with the final wedding preparations. As the ceremony would be at Hawksley she had somehow assumed the role of go-between, keeping Pru and Sarah up to date with what each woman was providing and organizing for the great day, about which they seemed more excited on occasions than Sophie herself. Dutifully she met the four little bridesmaids, who were really quite bearable as small girls go, approved their dresses, and at their insistence, solemnly practised at each visit her walk down the aisle, the little troop of four following her two by two and holding bunches of carrots in place of posies. It wasn't until the weekend in mid-November, when Ben was due to arrive home the following week in time for her twenty-first birthday that things started to feel wrong again.

She had left the manor later than usual on the Saturday. Sarah had asked her to stay until the Monday and she'd decided to delay leaving Hawksley for Kidlington after lunch. She was just finishing her breakfast when Tom came into the kitchen, his arms full of cream and gold hot house chrysanthemums.

'Thought you might like these for the drawing room,' he said, and set them on the kitchen side, 'I'm thinkin' it'll be the last of them for this year.'

'Thank you, Tom, they're lovely.' Carefully Sophie selected a half-dozen of the best blooms. Setting them on one side, she said, 'I'll take these to the churchyard this morning.'

'Arr.' Tom watched her in silence for a moment then said, 'Eli was there a day or so back and tidied away the old flowers, so them'll look fresh and make a right splash...ain't much colour around that old churchyard this time of year.'

'They are beautiful. ' She smiled. 'I thought I would like to take them my bridal bouquet after the wedding: make it their day as well.'

Tom moved to put his big arms around her. 'That's a right good thought, Sophie lass, and they'd be so proud to see you in all your finery.'

For a moment she rested her head against his, then stepped back and kissed his cheek. 'What would I do without you and Eli,' she said.

'Oh,' he flicked a gentle finger at her nose, 'No fear of us a-taking off. Me and Eli – we both fixtures around here 'till the day they carries us out feet first.' He gave a great rumble of laughter. 'An' I don't reckon that'll be someday soon!'

* * *

It was a cold morning, with misty droplets in the air and as she left the house Sophie took the scarf from around her neck to cover her hair, tying it loosely and tossing the ends back over her shoulders. She walked briskly, enjoying the quiet of early morning and the absence of visitors, although by the time she reached the village the main street was already busy and she stopped frequently to chat.

Like her mother, who, as the local people said: "Had never put on the airs and graces of some folk of her kind," Sophie had always been a part of village life, consequently she knew everyone and everyone knew her. Although from early childhood she'd never been keen on the "All Girls Together" gatherings, at Claire's gentle insistence she'd been a Brownie, and later, in Sophie's remembrance of her mother's wishes, a Guide with the local troop.

She'd also climbed trees and swum in the river with the boys, which had been much more fun, and along with both sexes of her peers, scrumped apples, ignored "No Trespass" notices and done all the verging-on-the-lawless things children do when out of sight and sound of adults; much as Rupert had done ten years before her. After the tragedy that had brought such devastation to her young life the people of Hawksley had opened their hearts to make Claire's daughter very much one of their own, closing ranks around her and helping in part to fill the awful yawning gap that the loss of both mother and brother had brought into her life.

When she eventually reached the churchyard it was like stepping into a different world, a silent world where the trees dripped mournfully and only the occasional bird ventured a soft cheep. As Sophie stooped to lay the flowers over the three graves she felt an odd little tremor along her spine and had a sudden notion that she was being watched. She laid the last flower and stood, giving herself a mental shake. *Don't be stupid,* she admonished silently, *churchyards do that to people!* Resisting the impulse to look over her shoulder she took off her scarf, shook out her hair, took a last look at the graves, then turning, walked away without venturing a backward glance.

'It was spooky,' she told Sarah later that day as they walked Archie, the family Springer, across the downs, 'honestly, I was sure someone was watching me; I did take a quick peek back just before I reached the gate but there was nothing out of the ordinary to see.'

Sarah laughed. 'Now if that had been Ben he would have jumped around, shouted "Ta Da!" and scared the life out of whosoever it was!'

'And felt a real idiot when there was no one there,' Sophie replied with a grin.

'Yes, well, there is that, I suppose,' Sarah said, and laughed again. 'Dear Sophie, only you would resist the temptation to peek.'

* * *

She enjoyed her week end with the Nicholls family; Sarah was warm and more relaxed now wedding preparations were almost complete, Hugh in an amiable mood and Julius was as always, alert and interested in all she had been doing at Hawksley since coming down from Oxford, and she spent long periods of time with him in his cosy sitting room, outlining her plans for the future.

'Not all the downstairs rooms have been open to the public,' she explained as they sat over an a glass of wine on her first evening, 'I think that next season we should open the whole ground floor, apart from the kitchens and pantry, the small sitting room-cum-study, Mrs Buckley's private quarters, and all those odd little rather grubby rooms at the back. When Ben and I move in properly, we can use the kitchen for most meals. The first floor of the main house will be more than adequate for us to rattle around in with enough spare rooms for any guests.' She paced the room, waving enthusiastic arms, 'I'd like to convert one of the extra downstairs rooms, perhaps the music room, or part of the long gallery, into a tea room...just for tea and cakes to begin with...I'm sure I can recruit some local ladies to work in shifts. If it takes off it might not make a fortune but if even only half the number of visitors use it should at least pay for itself...and might prove an added attraction,' she paused for breath. 'What do you think, papa?'

'I think my head is spinning!' he answered mildly. 'Now do sit down and let me hear how you propose to do all this in four short months.'

CHAPTER 6

Hampshire, November 1965

If Julius had reservations about how such things might be achieved, Ben, on hearing about Sophie's plans for Hawksley when he returned from his Australian trip, did not. By now he was beginning to know his beloved very well.

He had been aware from the very beginning that she had an inner strength and drive that wasn't always apparent to an outsider, even one as perspicacious as Julius. She was one of the most autonomous people Ben had ever met. In Sophie he knew he had the perfect foil for his rather more cautious approach to problems; someone who would always stand at his shoulder, not pushing, but urging him on: to believe in himself, to strive for what he wanted to achieve; and she would work alongside him to attain it, no matter how impossible it might seem to others.

In falling in love with Sophie, he had also he realised, found the other half of himself. This gave him a previously untapped instinct for what others were feeling, particularly Sophie; sometimes even for what she was thinking; although he wasn't always right in that respect, for Sophie's thoughts could be deep.

But on their first meeting at the manor after his return from Australia, he knew, despite the bright smile and eager arms with which she greeted him, that she definitely had something on her mind, and when dinner ended and Pru and Geoffrey had settled together before the drawing room fire, he drew her away into the chilly boot room, insisting she wrapped up warm before taking her hand and pulling her, a little unwilling, out into the frosty November night.

'It's freezing,' she protested, as they reached the terrace and descended onto the side lawn, 'and right now I'm in the mood for somewhere a little more cosy and intimate...my bedroom for instance.'

'Tsk, tsk,' he clicked his teeth. 'What a forward girl you are,' he disapproved, then wrapped his arms around her, hugging and kissing until she was breathless. 'There now – will that do until I can creep along the corridor after the witching hour and have my way with you?'

'I suppose it will have to, because I'm certainly not rolling around with you out here, even if I have been driven to the point of insanity with unfulfilled lust whilst you've been whooping it up Down Under.'

'Not much whooping,' he tucked her arm companionable in his as they began walking again. 'Actually, I plucked you from the bosom of your family so that you could spill what it is you've been dying to tell me ever since I arrived.'

'How do you know I've been dying to tell you anything?'

'Because that fact is lit up over your head in flashing neon lights,' he said. 'So come on: give; except' he added, 'if it's to confess you've been to bed with half the village rugby team whilst I've been away, I'd rather not know.'

'Idiot,' she said and paced on in silence for a few moments before asking, 'You remember that weekend I came home after we'd cleared the flat and there was a funny atmosphere about the place, with dad and Pru jumpy as hell?'

'Sure – but wasn't that over some nosey visitor?'

Sophie gave a derogatory sniff. 'Like hell it was. I know those two and it would take a lot more than someone straying onto private ground to rattle either of them all that much...' She frowned. 'Whatever it was it all seemed to die down until a couple of weeks after you'd left. I'd driven over to Kidlington for the weekend and when I came back on the Monday it was as though someone had taken a dirty great stick and stirred the whole the place up, leaving dad and Pru whizzing around like a couple of bluebottles under a jam jar and trying like mad to pretend everything was perfectly normal.'

She stopped again and turned to him. 'But, Ben, it was nothing like normal...I could *feel* it, and I wasn't the only one: Mrs Buckley had spent the Saturday night at her nieces' in Beaulieu, but when she came home on the Sunday afternoon and did her usual tour to see if there was any laundry to collect or tidying to do, she saw the blue room had been slept in. When she asked who'd stayed the night, Pru said *she'd* slept there; that she'd been restless and didn't want to disturb dad. But Mrs B says that was a bare-faced lie because there was a pair of men's hairbrushes, shaving soap and a used razor in the bathroom that hadn't been there before the weekend, so unless Pru had suddenly started to sprout whiskers, someone and a man at that, had stayed at least one night.'

'Perhaps it was an old Army pal of your fathers – or a relative of Pru's,' Ben suggested.

Sophie shook her head. 'Pru doesn't have any male relatives that I've ever heard of and never in all my life has any old army friend of dad's shown up...and that's not all,' she hesitated and stood for a moment, biting her lip. 'Look,' she said, 'if I tell you something, promise you won't laugh, because your mother did when I told her, and at the time I thought it was quite funny, but that was before all this other nonsense over the phantom visitor started. On the morning of the Saturday I was going over to Kidlington. I was just finishing breakfast when Tom brought in the last of the hothouse chrysanthemums and I decided to take some to put on Mother and Rupert and Grandma's graves...'

Ben listened in silence as she explained how she'd felt she wasn't alone in the churchyard; how reluctant she'd been to turn around and either confirm or deny there was someone else present. 'I just told myself not to be so stupid,' she said, and gave a little embarrassed laugh. 'And really, when I reached the gate and did finally look around there wasn't a sign of anyone lurking.' She forced a grin. 'Your mother said if it had been you in that situation you'd have jumped around, shouted "Ta Da!" and frightened the life out of whoever it might be.'

'I probably would have,' he said, 'and if I'd been wearing a mackintosh, I'd have flashed them as well!'

She laughed then, but sobered again almost immediately. 'That isn't all,' she said.' There's another thing...Rupert's album has disappeared, apparently into thin air. Before I left home to go to Oxford I'd begun to think there was something a little, well, unhealthy about keeping his room just as it was. In the beginning, when I was still a kid, it was a comfort for me to sit there sometimes, all on my own and think about him. Because of all the stairs Dad never went near it so I hadn't to worry it might upset him to find me there.'

She paused and gave a helpless little shrug. 'After I left school it began to feel too much like living in the past and all my interests then were centred on my future and getting to Oxford. Several times Pru and I discussed packing away all the books and bits and pieces and re-decorating the room, but never actually got around to it. When I came back that weekend to all the odd happenings and there was no you to talk to, I thought it might take my mind of things if I made a start, so after Pru and Dad had gone down to Stable cottage that afternoon I found an old trunk in the attic and began to clear all his things into it...' she paused again and turned her face to his, 'and Ben, everything in his desk was there, exactly as it had been for all these years...except for the album.'

'Are you sure?'

'If course I'm sure…it was always in the same place. Every time I'd looked at it I'd made certain I put it back right at the bottom of the drawer, beneath all the magazines and newspapers…I'll swear until then it had not been touched by anyone else since I first discovered it.'

'But you don't know for certain,' he said shrewdly, 'that you were the first one to find it, do you? After all, Rupert made that album before you were born; it's not unreasonable to suppose others might have seen it. He was only a little boy and I'd bet he couldn't wait to show it to *someone*.'

She was silent a moment; thinking, two vertical lines etched between her brows. 'N-o-o,' she said slowly. 'I just assumed…' She turned to him, 'You think my father knew about it, don't you?' she challenged.'

'Yes, I do.'

'But if he did why wait until now to move it?'

Ben's dark eyes held hers, and she saw there an answer to her question that made her catch her breath. 'The visitor,' she said, 'you think he took it to show the visitor.'

'When you think about it,' he said gently, 'it seems likely.'

'But…*why*?'

'Perhaps he thought he might be interested?'

Something was beginning to make sense in Sophie's sorely tried brain. She said slowly, choosing her words with care, 'I suppose whoever that visitor was might have been around here during the war…might even have been an American on holiday over here who knew the house and came back to take a look. I remember Mrs Buckley telling me how mother and my grandma held a big party here one New Year for some American flyers.' Her voice grew more certain. 'He might have been from one of the airfields around the Forest…he could even have known Rupert's Captain Pop.'

'He might,' Ben said reasonably, 'so why not ask your father outright? Surely it couldn't do any harm after all this time.'

'I can't,' she was aghast. 'You seem have forgotten: my brother's hero was more than likely my natural father. How could I possibly hurt Geoffrey by bringing that into the light of day now? He's my *dad*, Ben, and in a few weeks he'll walk me down the aisle and give me away in marriage…give me away as his daughter, which I am, far more than that of any dead American airman.'

Ben sighed and put his arms around her. 'Poor old you; your mother was right to tell you the truth from the beginning and I do understand how that terrible accident must have changed everything for your father…I know it's easy to be wise after the event but I can't help thinking how much better it would have been if all this web of secrecy and intrigue had never been spun. Your memory of your actual father and who he was should have been kept alive, made real to you, rather than sweeping him away under the carpet and never mentioning his name.'

She gave a wry little smile. 'But Rupert never forgot.'

'No, and that's his legacy to you.' Ben smoothed her hair and kissed the crown. 'One day, perhaps, someone will break the silence and you'll be able put a name to your brother's Captain Pop, and discover if he really was your father. But country people are loyal and if at the time everyone tacitly agreed that for his sake, and yours, it was better to keep schtum, that's what they did, and have continued to do ever since; better for now to keep looking to the future. As my father is always saying: "When one door closes, another opens,"' Ben turned her back towards the house. 'Let's keep everything that's happened these past weeks between us,' he said. 'We can take it out and dust it off and talk about it whenever you feel the need, but as my feet are now completely dead, possibly from frostbite, can we please leave it for now and get back to the fire?'

There was nothing like sharing one's troubles, Sophie mused, as she and Ben returned to the house. She was feeling considerably better and more cheerful now than she had been over the past couple of weeks. No harm had come of any of it, she comforted herself. Her lover was back; in two weeks she would be twenty-one and a few days after Christmas there would be no need for him to wait until the household and all but the two of them in it were fast asleep, before padding barefoot down the long corridor to her room.

The morning of her wedding dawned cold and clear and Sophie opened her curtains to an early sun that turned the frost-laden trees into a shimmering silver glory. Pushing open her window she caught the heady drift of wood smoke from the fires already lighted throughout the house. From now on all would be hustle and bustle, with extra hands hired from the village to clean and cook and prepare.

The Great Day was upon them at last.

It was the 29th December, 1965 and in a few hours she would become Mrs Sophie Nicholls. *Well,* she thought, *after all the alarms and excursions of the past weeks and a house full of guests over Christmas, it will be a relief to get it all over with, and for Ben and me to be on our own at last with only the future to think about.*

But still, a little worm of disquiet nibbled at the back of her mind;

raising an inquisitive head, nudging her sub-conscious into life, whispering: *someone was there, you know!*

She looked out across the sparkling morning. Were the watcher and the unknown visitor one and the same, and if so, then who might he have been...And why, when she'd finally got around to clearing Rupert's desk and adding its contents to the already half-filled trunk, had the album been back where it had always been: beneath the magazines and newspapers in the bottom drawer of his desk?

But there was little time for brooding over the events of the past week or so. First she had to dissuade Mrs Buckley from cooking the substantial breakfast the housekeeper deemed necessary to "settle her stomach," although as Sophie remarked later to Pru, a breakfast of bacon, egg and tomatoes was more likely to give her a massive dose of indigestion than do any settling. Coffee, a round of buttered toast and a long stroll around the gardens proved sufficient to calm the disturbing butterfly fluttering that would keep starting up around the region of her solar plexus at the thought of the day ahead.

Later, when the Nicholls family had arrived *en masse*, and Ben, with brother Guy, his best man, had been banished to the farthest end of the west wing lest he catch a glimpse of his bride before she arrived at the altar, Sophie began to wish they had made an earlier dash for Gretna Green. Although she suffered in silence the ministrations of Sarah and Pru as their joint fussing over her dress, hair and make-up brought her almost at screaming point, she held her impatience in check until everyone bar her father had departed and left her in peace. But when she descended the staircase into the great hall, now transformed with long tables positively groaning with food and drink, and saw her father leaning on his crutches, waiting alone at the foot of the stairs, the look in his eyes as she came towards him made it all worthwhile.

As Geoffrey took in the slender figure clothed in simple close fitting white satin, the tiara of diamonds holding the veil of sheer voile in place; he caught his breath and said softly, 'My darling girl; how proud Claire would have been to see you today.'

Sophie's eyes filled with tears and she put her arms around him. 'She couldn't be prouder than I am to have a dad like you to walk me down the aisle,' she said and for a moment she clung to him, realising for the first time what it meant to every father to let go of the past, say goodbye to his daughter and trust her future to another man.

'Tell you what,' Geoffrey gave her a sudden brisk kiss on the forehead. 'Now that crowd are all safely down at the church, how about we have a quick shot of single malt apiece?'

'Lovely idea, Dad, but won't it put Ben off to have his beloved arrive at the altar reeking of strong drink?

'He won't notice,' grunted Geoffrey, making for the side table laden with bottles, 'He was looking like a dying duck in a thunderstorm all morning so I gave him a stiff one just before he left!'

When the car arrived at Hawksley Church and as they made to pass through the lych gate, one of the many women clustered about the entrance called: 'Let's see your lovely face for a moment, m'dear – I'm due at work in ten minutes and won't be here to see you come out wi' your veil lifted!'

Sophie let go of her father's arm and putting her hands beneath the veil swept it up, holding it over the small silver tiara for a moment before letting it drop back over her laughing face. The crowd gave an appreciative cheer as she laid her hand on her father's arm again, and with Geoffrey moving carefully on his crutches, walked the short pathway to the church door and her waiting bridesmaids.

As the church doors opened and the organ thundered into life, Ben and his brother turned as one from the altar rail to watch Sophie's progress towards them. At that sudden vision of loveliness Ben was momentarily too overcome to manage more than a huge, and very audible gulp of relief and joy, while beside him an awestruck Guy, his normally saturnine face split into a wide grin, hissed: 'Oh, my God...will you just look at that, you jammy so-and-so!'

The waiting vicar gave a discreet disapproving cough and they both hastily did an eyes-front. Ben heard the whisper of Sophie's dress as she reached his side and turning again, ventured a smile. Beneath the sheer veil his bride closed one eye in a slow wink and his heart turned. The vicar coughed again, waited a moment then began: 'Dearly beloved, we are gathered here today....'

It was a pity, Sophie thought, that they couldn't do it all again; the whole ceremony had proceeded so much more quickly than the previous day's rehearsal that she couldn't help feeling she may have missed out on some of it. In no time at all it seemed, the register had been signed, kisses exchanged all round, the organist was pulling out all the stops for Mendelssohn's hysterical Wedding March and she was walking back down the aisle between the serried ranks of beaming friends and relations: Mrs Benjamin Daniel Julius Nicholls, her mother-in-law having had her exclusive say in the naming of her second son.

'I know it's a bit of a mouthful,' he'd said, when she'd exploded into giggles on hearing his full name, 'but who are you to snigger at me when you'll have to stand up in church and admit to being Sophie Francesca Claire de Lacy!

They reached the door of the church and stepped into the winter sunlight; just the two of them, the eager little bridesmaids held back by parents, and for those first few seconds as the photographer aimed his camera, Sophie and Ben stood alone; Ben looking sideways at his bride, Sophie smiling as she let her eyes rove first from Ben's face, then over the waiting crowds before turning her gaze automatically towards the churchyard, where her mother, her brother Rupert, and grandma, Marion de Lacy, slept.

Almost invisible in the shadows of the great Yew stood two figures and as she watched, the taller moved a half step forward out of the shadows. Even at that distance, and for the space of a single a heartbeat, Sophie's gaze met eyes of a startling, azure blue; then Geoffrey and Pru and a dozen guests were around them and almost deafened by the cries of the waiting well-wishers, she was swept forward with Ben into a hail of confetti,.

When she looked again the figures were gone, only the Yew, magnificent in age, stood alone and brooding over the quiet churchyard.

That night, as they lay drowsy from lovemaking, she told Ben about it. He was silent for a long minute then: 'There were two people, you think?' he asked

'Yes; I'm, almost sure. I wouldn't have noticed them at all if the man hadn't moved; I couldn't see either of them clearly...I probably wouldn't have noticed them at all if the he hadn't looked straight at me; I didn't have time to register anything much else about him as everyone suddenly shot out of the church like corks out of a bottle; only that he was tall, wore one of those Anthony Eden hats and had the brightest blue eyes I've ever seen.'

'Most likely they were just a couple of visitors who were wandering around the graveyard reading the tombstones,' he said comfortingly. 'Some people do that, you know. They must have thought it quite a bonus to be onlookers at a wedding.'

'I daresay you're right,' Sophie yawned. 'Anyway, I'm sure he wasn't anyone I know.' She yawned again and snuggled closer. 'But he did have the most wonderful blue eyes...'

CHAPTER 7

Italy and France, January, 1966

They spent the first week of their honeymoon in Florence and after three days of viewing art galleries and churches, decided to give culture and their feet a break, instead spending the daylight hours exploring the small twisting streets, the houses with ancient frescos over the lintels; tiny out of the way café's and smoky cellar bars serving pasta and good Italian wines. Although it was cold, the weather was dry and bright and on most mornings they sat at a pavement table on the piazza, warmed by the pale winter sun, drinking coffee before the ornate and improbable wedding cake edifice of San Croc.

Julius had been disbelieving when they announced their honeymoon destination. "For why should you want to go to Florence in winter?" he demanded. "You want cold, you should go to the Italian Alps, or to Switzerland or Austria, where snow is of some use other than for freezing your feet!"

Ben had chuckled. "Too many people on the slopes in January," he'd replied, "and nobody much in Tuscany – we want to get away from everyone for a while, papa."

"And after Florence," put in Sophie, "we go by train to Siena for a few days before flying to Tours to see Dominic – Ben insists I meet him before he comes here to look at our land and see what vines we should have and how many."

Mollified, the old man had nodded sagely over the last. "And he will sell them to you from his own vineyard." he had paused then and looked slyly at Sophie, "He has such a head for business for a *goyim*, but for you he will make a fair price."

"What Papa means," Ben had countered with a grin, "is that he's a shrewd business man and very susceptible to a pretty face; of which weaknesses I'll take full advantage when it comes to bargaining with him for our vines!"

* * *

When they arrived in Siena it was snowing; not much, but the mere inch of snow had frozen overnight, making walking hazardous and putting all but the hardiest visitors off any idea of sight-seeing.

51

Sophie and Ben, so recently married, were quite happy to spend the mornings in bed and the afternoons in the hotel lounge watching cartoons and incomprehensible Italian films on Television, with an occasional American epic dubbed into Italian. As the dubbing of the latter was invariably out of sync with the actors lip movements they were frequently reduced to laughter that at times verged on the hysterical. After one such evening they stumbled back up to bed, giggling helplessly and holding onto each other like drunken sailors.

Sophie couldn't remember behaving quite so badly before in the whole of her life, but it was fun and all the extra hours spent in bed a definite bonus.

'I'm not sure I like the sound of your M'sieur de la Tour,' she said as they boarded the 'plane which would fly them to Tours, 'it's all right for you; you've known him for years but I'm not all that keen on spending the last few days of our honeymoon with a stranger.'

Ben grinned. 'You shouldn't take any notice of what Papa Julius says; he was just winding you up. Dominic's one of the best; he's only a couple of years older than me but he just happens to have had a lot more girlfriends than anyone else I know...they buzz around him like bees around a hive. But you'll be quite safe, darling; we won't be staying with him as his cottage is much too small.'

'Shame; I was just beginning to get interested,' she was gently mocking and he squeezed her hand.

'We'll be with his parents, who have a whacking great place a few miles out of the city and only a stone's throw from the vineyard. You'll like Charles and Caro de la Tour – probably even more than you'll like Dom – who isn't really their son.' Ben added nonchalantly as they buckled themselves into their seatbelts. 'In fact, the family background is something on a par with your own, so you and Dom should have a lot in common.'

'It's just like you to leave it until the last minute to tell me the important things about people,' Sophie grumbled. 'May I ask *why* we should all have a lot in common?'

'Missing parents,' he answered. 'I don't know the whole story; just that he was the result of an affair in nineteen-forty between his mother and an unknown German soldier. Lise was Charles' cousin and barely sixteen, he was ten years older, but he married her to save her reputation, then immediately afterward went underground with the resistance.'

'Not very gallant of him, was it?' Sophie was sarcastic, 'leaving his pregnant bride like that.'

'Well, it was hardly a love match and he *could* have stayed single and left her to the mercy of the townswomen, who would have made her life hell for fraternizing with a German.'

'I suppose you have a point there. What happened to Lise then?'

Ben shrugged. 'Not sure. Caro told me once that she died during the war while Charles was with the Free French in England doing something murky with the SAS. The child apparently just disappeared somewhere in France and wasn't found until a couple of years after the war – in a convent orphanage in Ireland, of all places, by which time Charles, who'd been an architect before the war, had married Caro and they were living on her father's flower farm in Cornwall. I think it was Caroline who found Dominic just as they were about to leave Cornwall and move to Chartres where Charles was joining his old firm and where they lived for a few years until Charles set up his own business in Tours.'

'So his father isn't his father and his mother isn't his mother.' Sophie was both intrigued and sympathetic. 'Poor chap; I don't suppose he even remembers her; he must have been very young when she died.'

'Um,' Ben settled back into his seat. 'But he's a big boy now' he said, 'so don't go feeling too sorry for him… he does have rather a lost look about him sometimes.' He made big soulful eyes at her and added, 'that's probably why all the girls fall for him!'

Dominic stood patiently waiting in the airport arrivals hall. Leaning on the metal barrier, letting his gaze rove over the passengers from Flight 17 as they began surging into the hall, he noticed the girl almost immediately; one could hardly miss her, he thought – she stood out a mile from the crowd, her blonde head shining silver under the shafts of sunlight streaming from the high windows, the fantastic, sculptured lines of her face, the lithe body and lovely, swinging walk of her – it was only as she drew nearer and became more detached from the crowd that he saw she was not alone, but walking hand in hand with…he gave a wry shrug and let go the breath he had been holding…with his good friend, Ben Nicholls.

Merde! Just my luck! He straightened, pasting a welcoming smile onto his face, and as Ben's seeking glance connected with his own, raised a long arm in greeting. Ben waved back and turned to speak to the beautiful one, who looked directly at Dominic before unleashing a wide smile that did something quite unbelievable to his libido.

'There he is,' Ben squeezed Sophie's hand, '– on the left at the end of the barrier.'

Sophie looked across the hall and immediately locked eyes with a tall, rangy, man, who gazed back at her with an intense dark-eyed stare. Although conventionally dressed in black slacks and black turtle neck sweater under a hip length tan leather jacket, in some subtle way he stood out from the crowd. When he returned her involuntary smile, his whole face lit up, so than one failed to register that apart from the long lashed eyes and the smile, he was by no means a handsome man; although he had a wide brow and thick abundant dark hair, his face was too thin for handsome; his skin lined and tanned from long days spent working under summer suns and toughened by the bitter winds of winter.

But good looking or not, Sophie felt an immediate flutter somewhere beneath her ribs and caught her breath. *My God*, she thought, no *wonder he pulls the girls*...then Ben was laughing and drawing her forward, saying, 'Close your mouth, Dom...Let me introduce you: this is my wife, Sophie; Sophie, meet Dominic de la Tour.'

He bent over her hand with a murmured '*Enchante,* Sophie. Welcome to Tours.'

She said, 'Thank you, I'm very pleased to be here at last, Dominic.'

He shook Ben's hand vigorously. 'My old friend; how good it is to see you...' He turned again to Sophie. 'This one,' he said, 'has always had such luck in life...me, I must work in the fields like a peasant while he has a nice job in a warm office...' he spread his hands, 'and now he comes to visit with such a beautiful wife.'

'Peasant, my eye,' Ben winked at Sophie. 'He's got nothing to complain about; *he* could have had a had a nice job in a warm office with his papa, instead he drove Charles crazy until he let him leave the Sorbonne and work in a vineyard...and God knows, he's had the pick of enough gorgeous girls.'

'But,' said Dominic, hefting one of their cases and leading them out of the terminal towards the car park, 'not one of them could cook as well as my mama, nor were they as beautiful as your Sophie...so, still I am the bachelor!'

'I don't cook all that well,' confessed Sophie and Ben slipped an arm about her waist.

'Who cares,' he said.

* * *

The four days spent in the de la Tour family home passed all too

54

quickly. Only a year or two older than Ben, Dominic was a relaxed, easy-going man and his parents, Charles and Caroline, welcoming and practised hosts. Their house, a substantial mansion a few miles out of the city, had a long garden running down to the Loire, where a smart motor launch rocked gently at a landing stage. 'Too cold at present for river trips,' Caroline had apologised with a smile, at Sophie's involuntary exclamation of delight, 'but you must come again later in the year when our daughter, Hélène, is home from her studies. Then we'll take a picnic and have a day out, just we three women, and show you the sights along the Loire.'

Sophie notched that up as something to look forward to. Caro was a lively, shrewdly intelligent, pretty woman in her late thirties who appeared to move smoothly through life, plainly adored by her stepson and the more than averagely handsome Charles, from whom his not quite legitimate son had obviously inherited the family dark, long-lashed come-to-bed eyes, caressing voice and sexy smile.

It was a lovely, peaceful interlude in that old house by the river, interspersed with busy days at the vineyard; sitting in Dominic's little stone built cottage pouring over the plans that Ben and his grandfather had drawn up together for the Hawksley meadow; discussing the price and type of grape that would do best in the chalky Hampshire soil, and when Dominic would visit to see the land for himself before coming over to assist with the planting in early spring. But as they prepared to board their flight home they were both aware that once settled back at Hawksley, although life might indeed continue to be peaceful, for the foreseeable future at least it would be unlikely to be leisurely to any noticeable degree.

Dominic had driven them to the airport and when they left to board their plane, hurried to the observation tower to watch it take off, but even when the aircraft was no more than a speck in the wide blue sky he continued to lean on the balcony rail of the observation lounge and stare towards the empty horizon.

Sophie...the name had a magical sound for him; he savoured it on his tongue. *Soph-ie.* He gave his wry, turned down smile. He was twenty-seven, verging on twenty-eight years old; had almost loved several women; even thought he might have been in love with one or two, but never known what love was until now, or how much it could hurt. *Too late, too late:* the two people to whom he had just made his farewells were so much, so obviously, radiantly in love, and he had, as his old friend Ben would say: "Missed the Boat".

Sophie Nicholls was as lost to him as if they had never met.

Dominic finally turned away and made his way out of the airport and back to his car. As he drove towards home, to his familiar little cottage by the vineyard he wondered how he would manage future meetings with his good friend Ben's beautiful wife. For meetings there must be; he had promised his support in setting up Ben's vineyard and there would be many visits he must make in the coming year or two to this unknown and as yet unseen Hawksley Manor.

Ben was as a brother to him; they had met as children when Julius Berger toured the French vineyards after the war to broker deals for wine. When he had met Charles de la Tour by accident at one of the vineyards, it was a meeting that over the years became a close and valued friendship. With the ties between the two families so strong and deep for Dominic to make any move to seduce Sophie away from Ben, even if she proved seducible, which he was sure she would not, was unthinkable. He would just have to hide his feeling at future meetings and learn to live with the pain of unrequited love.

Sophie leaned her head against Ben's shoulder at take-off to avoid the temptation of peeping to see if Dominic was watching from the observation deck. The warmth of her husband's body seeping through his tweed jacket comforted and reassured her. She knew Ben was the only man for her but Dominic had proved something of a distraction and she was glad their meetings had always been in the company of others: there was something dangerous about him…not in the way a homicidal maniac was dangerous, she thought, with a sudden inward giggle; *his* danger lay in a subtle magnetism and charm, to which she had no doubt many women had succumbed. She did, she acknowledge honestly, find him attractive, even disturbing, but she did not need the charm or charisma of any Dominic de la Tour to make her heart beat faster; she already had Ben, her beloved, who could do that, and *he* was all she would ever want or need.

Ben was content to sit with Sophie's head on his shoulder, watching the ground rush by as the aircraft lifted and began to climb. He hadn't missed the expression in Dominic's eyes every time they rested on Sophie, nor had he missed her involuntary little catch of the breath and flush at her first meeting with his friend; nor the fact that Dominic had stood today and watched their plane leave, something he had never done for Ben alone. Thinking about those little tell-tale signs of attraction between them he was aware of a quick stab of jealousy. What might he do, he mused, half in jest, half in earnest, if the unthinkable happened and he found they had become lovers –

56

murder Dominic? – Possibly. Do the same to Sophie? Never! But too many of those smouldering looks from the bugger and he'd give Dominic de la Tour something to think about. His knuckles itched and his chest tightened. Sophie raised her head.

'What are you brooding about?'

'Nothing,' he rubbed his chin on her head. 'What do you think of Dominic now you've had a chance to know him?'

Sophie yawned. 'He's all right,' she said and added provocatively: 'but if I was going for anyone it would be Charles...talk about sex-appeal, if I was Caro I'd fit that one with a ball and chain!'

There were times, Ben thought, when he could really contemplate giving her a smack; not hard, just a little one perhaps...

PART TWO

1971–1982

THE YEARS BETWEEN

When I remember bygone days
I think how evening follows morn;
So many I loved were not yet dead,
So many I love were not yet born.

Ogden Nash

CHAPTER 8

Hampshire September 1971

Sophie opened wide the bedroom window and leaning out, took a deep breath of the late September air: a little sharp, with the first hint of frosty mornings to come, but bright with sunshine, the small cotton wool clouds almost motionless in the blue sky. She gave a relieved, heartfelt sigh; an Indian Summer, or as some still called it, St. Giles' Little Summer, had served them well this year in lingering on to provide a perfect day for their first real, wine-making harvest.

Ben had been up since dawn. Too impatient to stay in bed until a civilized hour, he had rousted Dominic from his own slumbers and could now be heard beneath the window, talking earnestly with Dominic, Tom and Eli. Sophie leaned further out over the sill until she could just see the tops of four heads bent close together: Ben's dark curls, Dominic's sleek brown poll, Eli's tow head, Tom's now familiar Hooray Henry check cap covering his prematurely thinning locks. About to call a morning greeting she was distracted by the sound of two pairs of feet running along the landing, heralding the twins, who needed no excuse to be up early on any morning, save when an unlawful consumption of unripe strawberries had laid both low for a day or two that summer with what Ben had called the Bombay Trots.

Jamie hurtled into the room and onto the bed a fraction before Alexander, where both proceeded to wrestle energetically amid the rumpled bedclothes. 'All right, all right; that's enough.' Sophie left the window to sit on the side of the bed, holding out her arms and letting both boys scramble into them. She ruffled their hair; one blonde, one dark, and smiled down into two pairs of laughing eyes: one pair brown, the other sapphire blue, and thought again that not having identical twins really was a bonus; unlike some doubly harassed mothers she could tell them apart and they had such disparate temperaments that the actions of one could never be confused with those of the other: the dark James Geoffrey, eager, mercurial, always on the move; Alexander Julius, the younger by a bare three minutes, blonde, calmer, thoughtful and easy going, although always ready to join in any mischief making, or indeed any pursuits, lawful or unlawful his twin might devise.

It had come as a not altogether welcome surprise to discover the carefree, and it had to be admitted, sometimes careless nights she and Ben had spent in Italy had resulted in the arrival of these two premature bundles of joy that following September.

It had certainly put on hold for a year most of her plans for increasing the opening of the house to visitors from two to five days a week and dispensing with the professional guides, but somehow during the years following the twin's birth, a comfortable, homely cafe, supplied with cakes and scones and sandwiches and run by a rota of willing helpers of both sexes from the village, had been created in the old music room; the house spruced up, mainly by Ben wielding a paintbrush during intervals between preparing the big meadow for the vines and all that entailed, and Sophie fitting in the business side of both projects between washing down paintwork, overseeing the creation of the cafe and taking over a half of the guided tours. It had been an exhausting but exciting few years during which Julius made several visits, each time throwing up his hands in astonishment and heaping admiration and congratulations on them for their industry.

In the early days the babies were transported around the work areas in Moses baskets, then later taken in hand by Mrs Buckley's sixteen year old niece, Daisy, who wanted to train as a children's nurse and with whom they formed a mutual admiration society. By the time Daisy finally departed to Salisbury Hospital to begin her training the boys had found their feet and were settled happily, trailing their parents around the house out of season, and when visitors were around settled either with their willing grandparents at Stable cottage, or with Mrs Buckley in the kitchen, or out in the grounds 'helping' Tom and Eli in the myriad tasks around the orchard and gardens the former farm hands had taken on since the sale of the Home Farm.

Altogether, life was good, if at times exhausting and the first harvest from their vineyard a high point for excitement and celebration. Julius would arrive later that morning, by which time Ben, herself, Dominic, Tom, Eli and a half dozen student helpers from the nearby Agricultural College would be well into filling their pails with the harvest.

By the time she had hustled the boys through a quick bath and into their shirts, warm jerseys and dungarees, supervised the laborious fastening of shoes and helped Mrs Buckley in providing breakfast for everyone, the students had arrived and the real work of the day could begin.

It was a day to recall with joy and talk over on winter evenings to come. For the rest of her life Sophie would remember holding the first bunch of tight white grapes in her palm, then cutting the fibrous stem and dropping the firm cluster into the bucket slung over one arm, and when that was full, tipping it into the crates on the trailer as the tractor trundled slowly between the long rows of vines. Remember most poignantly Ben's laughter; his face glowing with a mixture of pride and delight in what they had achieved together, and whenever they met during their labours he would give her a wide smile that said it all: *We did it, Soph: we really did it!* And she would smile back, her eyes answering: *Yes, you crazy cock-eyed optimist, we certainly did!*

Much later that evening, both boys in bed; Tom, Eli and the students returned to their various domiciles, the evening meal finished and cleared, in the cooling evening they sat on the long rear terrace in the old rattan chairs that had been there since Sophie's childhood: Dominic leaning forward occasionally to pluck and sniff at the wild thyme growing between the cracks in the paving, while Ben and Sophie nursed hands sore and aching from the concentrated hard labour of wielding secateurs and heaving boxes. Julius, warmly cocooned in a woollen plaid rug sat enthroned in their midst on his favourite carver chair fetched from the dining hall for the occasion, smoking his pipe and smiling benignly on them all.

'In time to come,' he said, 'you will remember only the triumph of your first harvest...and forget all those obstacles you must overcome before this day.'

'Like the amount of time it took to plant the vines,' Ben said feelingly.

'And hammer the stakes and string the wires,' Sophie added, 'and put all those rabbit guards over the saplings only to have the little beasts push them all up and have a feast; after that problem was solved and the plants were growing well the deer came and played havoc with the lot!'

Everyone laughed, but at the time it had been no laughing matter. An eight foot high fence had been needed around the entire vineyard to keep the deer at bay: a hideously expensive and back-breaking task and despite the combined efforts of Ben, Tom and Eli to do it themselves, an expert fencer had needed to be engaged and paid for.

Sophie lay back in her chair feeling warm and safe; closing her eyes she gave a little squeeze to Ben's fingers laced with hers. Seated as she was between the two younger men she was all too aware of Dominic on her other side and sought the reassuring feel of Ben's answering comfortable pressure on her own fingers. Somehow, even

63

if they were twelve feet apart in a room filled with other people, she still found the mere presence of Dominic disturbing. There was nothing romantic about this involuntary response to his appearance. She was totally bonded to Ben as he to her and there was no room in her heart for anyone else; even a man as undoubtedly attractive and charismatic as her husband's best friend, but none of that prevented her heart beating just a little bit too fast when he was about. He would, she thought with mingled relief and regret, be gone again in a day or two, then perversely wished he could stay longer.

Over the past three years there had been many of these fleeting visits; never lasting more than a few days, made to check on the vines and go into long intense conversational huddles with Ben. In turn, she and Ben would spend a week at the time in France and there had been more than one of the promised river trips with Caroline de la Tour and her daughter, Hélène. Sophie always looked forward to these visits; she had felt an immediate bond with Caro, as she liked to be called, and Hélène was almost a carbon copy of her mother...the same curling brown hair, the same warm complexion and sparkling green-grey eyes. On these visits, surrounded as she was by the de la Tour family, she had felt cushioned against the disturbing presence of the son of the house.

Dominic leaned to pluck another piece of thyme from the paving, rubbing it between his palms before inhaling the scent. From his stooping position he saw Ben and Sophie's entwined fingers and his mouth twitched in an involuntary wry smile. He glanced quickly away, only to be caught in the contemplative stare of Julius's beady black eyes. The old man held his gaze for a long moment before giving a slow, knowing smile and raising an enquiring eyebrow.

Again, Dominic looked away. Were his feelings that obvious? Tomorrow, he vowed silently he would make an excuse to leave early. After all, the first precious harvest was in; the fruits of it already on the way to the winery near Ringwood; there was no longer any real reason for him to stay. It would be a wrench but better perhaps for them all if he left first thing in the morning...

Oh dear, Julius gave a little sigh, so that was how the land lay!

He sat back in his chair; raising his hands he placed his fingertips together, watching over his spectacles the two people who were closest to his heart as they sat contentedly, hands entwined, blissfully oblivious of either his thoughts or those of Dominic. And yet...Julius sharpened his gaze: was it only his grandson who seemed unaware...

was the lovely Sophie not a little flushed this evening; did her fingers not clasp her husband's a little too tightly? He sighed again: foolish of him not to acknowledge that for some time he had been aware of a faint but unmistakable *frisson* in the air whenever she and the young Frenchman were together. He sighed again. Nothing to do about it but trust to the strength of Sophie's love for Ben and Dominic's loyalty to his friend to keep such mutual attraction within bounds.

He stole a sideways look at his grandson's face; saw the slight tic jump at his temple...always a sign of tension; sometimes of the anger, nowadays well controlled, that had on occasions flashed in childhood and adolescence.

Young Dominic, Julius thought, had better watch his step and avoid having that anger unleashed against himself...

* * *

That first harvest at Hawksley marked the beginning of many changes; some slow and subtle, others more immediate, the chief one of the latter being that Dominic no longer visited several times a year, and on the infrequent occasions he did, stayed only a day or two before travelling on to Cornwall, ostensible to see his adoptive grandparents. Sophie, although relieved in a way that her life was now less complicated by her sometimes confused and confusing feelings towards him, still missed his company, although strangely Ben, wrapped up as he now was in the vineyard and all its many mixed problems and pleasures, appeared not to notice the infrequency of his friend's visits. The fact that he, Sophie and the twins were invited without fail to spend their holiday each summer with the de la Tour family, when he could talk wine by the hour with Dominic, seemed sufficient contact now for her husband, but Sophie missed their friend's presence; missed his unfailing, laid back good humour, his wry grin and the warmth in his dark eyes when they met hers.

But it was better this way, she told herself firmly; less complicated and much less disturbing – and didn't she have enough to do with the twins and the house and all the changes she was making, had to make, to keep the Manor a going concern? The wine was proving popular and in a few more years when it became more established and accepted on its own merits, should more than repay all their hard work. Not that she worried about that aspect: with a father and brother-in-law in the wine trade, Hawksley Manor Sparkling Wine would in the fullness of time be on the wine list of every good restaurant from Land's End to John o' Groats.

65

In the meantime, finding the ways and means to keep a roof over their heads was mainly up to her...

CHAPTER 9

Hawksley Manor, January 1974

It was frosty, with a distinct nip in the air and the last thing most of workforce wanted to do was turn out on a cold January morning to prune the vines – apart from the twins, who wrapped up in duffle coats, scarves and gloves were enthusiastic recruits for the picking-up and bagging the resultant debris of pruning, although even that enthusiasm would no doubt pall as the day progressed.

While Sophie, along with the three strapping sons Tom and Eli had produced between them were lingering over large mugs of steaming coffee, Ben, who relished every moment in the great outdoors and was relentlessly full of *joie de vive,* left his own coffee half-finished and boyish face alight with enthusiasm urged them to: 'Come on, now – all hands to the pump and with luck we'll get at least half the job finished today.'

'And end up with frostbite and hypothermia, no doubt,' commented Sophie dryly as she relinquished her own coffee and pulled on stout leather gloves. 'OK, Simon Legree...lead on, the slaves are ready – more or less.'

She was an old hand at pruning now, and while she snipped at the tough stems of the vines to defeat both the cold and mind-numbing boredom of the task, she let her mind drift towards just how she was going to present her updated and somewhat ruthless plans for the future of the manor to her father and Pru; Ben she knew would back her up, even if he might think her plan too radical by a mile, but Geoffrey she was sure wouldn't like it, not one little bit; would probably fight her, tooth and nail. However, when he had made the manor over to herself and Ben he had in effect given them a free hand and the ultimate decision was for her and Ben to make.

It was ridiculous to have more than half the rooms closed and unheated through the winter months, the furniture shrouded in dust sheets. Such conditions did nothing for the fabric of the building and the effort needed to keep the encroaching damp at bay was a perpetually nagging reminder that while the vineyard flourished where the house was concerned they were not moving forward but merely just marking time, and in some respects, losing ground.

She had given endless hours of thought to the problem; a realist, she knew there was a limit to how long she could keep up with the relentless pressures of her multiple duties as organiser and part time tour guide through the summer months when the house was open to the public, coupled with her all year round role as wife and support to Ben and mother to their two growing young boys. In a few more years Mrs Buckley would be thinking about retirement and buying a house by the sea with her younger sister; when that time came it would be a terrible blow to everyone at Hawksley, particularly to Sophie, who had never know a time without that warm, reassuring and practical presence to turn to in times of trouble.

She paused for a moment to massage her aching right hand and call to the twins, who were becoming bored and showing a tendency to wander off; wandering off usually meant mischief and with everyone so busy it was safer to keep them occupied in some way or another. When they somewhat reluctantly reached her side she slipped them each a chocolate toffee and sent them off to visit grandma and grandpa. Tough on Pru and Geoffrey, she thought with a private grin, but as Pru was always saying, and meaning, "That's what grandparents are for!" Sophie was only too pleased to take advantage from time to time. As healthy active nine years olds both boys could get into mischief at the proverbial drop of a hat. Tomorrow, thank heaven, they would be back at the village school, returning at the end of each day ravenously hungry and once the inner man had been satisfied, ready to race their matchbox cars in the long galley before curling up in front of the fire with a book apiece. With a bit of luck they would forget all about switching on the TV until the mindless cartoons were over and it was time for a more innocuous and healthy *Blue Peter* or *Out of Town*...

Mechanically she resumed her task whilst her mind continued to marshal the facts and figures, the persuasive arguments she must have ready before she took the next momentous step. This evening when the house was quiet and Jamie and Alexander in bed, Ben and herself plus Tom, Eli and Mrs Buckley – because she needed those three trusty friends as well as Ben with whom to share her ideas and be on her side if her plans were to succeed – would sit and relax around the kitchen table and talk things through.

* * *

'You want to sell off part of the Manor to strangers?' Ben sounded as incredulous as he looked. He rumpled his hair much in the manner of Stan Laurel and gazed at her in comical disbelief, 'How on earth can you do that?'

'Not sell, rent,' Sophie was calm, matter of fact. 'I've done my homework these past months and I think it's a perfectly viable plan.'

'Then what would happen to all them visitors if you'm filled the place wi' tenants, may I ask?' queried Tom, peering at Sophie with one of his famous, *I'm just a poor gormless old sod and don't have a clue what you're talking about,* expressions on his weather-beaten face.

They were seated around the kitchen table with mugs of coffee and slices of warm gingerbread; the latest in a long line of manor cats dozed on the range while the old mahogany framed schoolroom clock on the wall measured the seconds with a muted *tick* and a louder *TOCK*. Roomy but cosy, the kitchen was a favourite place in which to discuss everything to do with the house and what remained of the estate. Over the years many conferences, some lasting until the small hours, had taken place around the long pine table.

Mrs Buckley stirred her coffee with great deliberation and quelled Tom with a look. 'Suppose we all hear Miss Sophie out before we starts looking for trouble,' she said, and nodded at Sophie. 'Go on, my dear, we're all listening.'

Sophie took a deep breath. 'My plan is that the great hall, most of the West wing, which of course includes the cafe and four of the first floor bedrooms – and the grounds, would remain open to the public as usual. *We* would continue to keep for our own use the main part of the house beyond the hall...this kitchen, sitting room, the snug for the boys, the old library cum office and of course, Bucky dear, your own apartment on the ground floor. While the house is open to the public we'd continue to use the old staff staircase off this kitchen to our bedrooms and bathrooms on the first floor, keeping the main staircase as the access to the first for the visitors, then once the house is closed we claim it back!'

'Nothing new there, then,' commented Ben, 'so OK Soph; what happens to the East wing and the extra bedrooms you're counting out of the tour in the West?'

'We take the East wing out of the public domain altogether, which gives us ten rooms of assorted sizes on the ground floor, plus the two cloakrooms we put in – we'll replace those with a proper brick built toilet block by the car park; the eight rooms and two bathrooms on the upper floor would become three apartments with modern kitchens and up to date bathrooms. At the same time we rearrange those spare bedrooms and bathrooms in the West into two more self-contained apartments. The existing side entrances to the service stairs from the courtyard in each wing would be widened to give access to the upper and lower levels, making them private from the rest of the house and visitors.'

Ben was cautious. 'Sounds all right but suppose we commission all that work and no one *wants* to rent?'

There was a murmur of agreement from Tom and Eli and Sophie paused before producing her trump card. 'I said I'd done my homework.' She held up the fingers of her right hand and began to count them off one by one. 'The Greys over at Rochford House have already done it with great success; also Tim Murrayfield at Ragbourne Hall. Nancy and Gordon Vine at The Grange at Beaulieu had prospective tenants waiting for all *ten* of their apartments before they were even completed, while at Fordingbridge John Russell converted the whole of Cold Ash into apartments and moved his family into the Dower House. I know all this because while you were off hob-nobbing in France with Dominic last autumn, I was doing a fact-finding tour around a few fallen-on-hard times and now doing-very-nicely old country estates.'

Sophie paused to let her word sink in before reaching for Ben's hand and adding gently. 'Darling, I don't want to share Hawksley with strangers either, but unless one has a place as massive and famous with Royal connections such as Broadlands, that can host affairs like big agricultural shows and up-market weddings, smaller old manor houses like ours have no alternative but to adapt and change to survive.

'Seems like there should be some other way of keepin' the place private, like,' Tom shifted uncomfortably. 'Don't know as I can quite see it working.'

'Oh, Tom,' Sophie raised her shoulders in a despairing gesture. 'Don't think I haven't explored other possibilities – as a last resort many old county families in financial trouble are turning their houses over to the National Trust so that they can remain *in situ* as tenants and tour guides at a peppercorn rent. I don't know about you, but I don't want that for Hawksley; I want *something* left to hand over to our sons.'

'Well,' Eli put down his coffee cup with a decisive click. 'I'm thinking that's one damned good idea on paper – an' so will this brother o' mine when he's 'ad time to think about it...but rather you than me to sell it to 'is 'ighness!' and he gave Sophie a broad wink.

Ben was still cautious. 'Before we get too carried away; what's it all likely to cost?'

'Not as much as you might think – and thanks to Julius' help and your hard work, along with Tom and Eli here in turning the vineyard into a well-established and profitable business we do have a healthy bank balance. The bulk of money dad gave us when we were married has been sitting around accruing interest for the past ten years and should be more than enough to pay for the plans we'll need to have properly drawn up and the materials and workforce to carry them out.'

Eli gave a huge grin. 'Well, my boy Charlie's a plumber, in't he, so that's one man hired at no fancy rates!'

Sophie laughed. 'And the twin's best friend at school's dad's an architect, so that's another!'

'It's a lot to take in at one go, but I don't see why it can't be done.' Ben squeezed Sophie's hand. 'I trust you, my love; I don't know where you got your drive and business acumen from but I'll back you any day – and all the way, but by God, you'll have a job on your hands if you expect to bring Geoffrey around to the idea without a fight.'

'He'll hate it,' agreed the housekeeper, 'but, you know, Mr. Ben; tucked away like he is in Stable Cottage, it shouldn't disturb him one little bit…and it will bring a lot more life to the place…a shame, I've always thought, to have all them lovely rooms shut away like they have been for half the year.'

Sophie looked around at the circle of familiar and much loved faces. 'Well,' she said, and raised her mug, 'then that's settled. So let's drink to the future and a new chapter in the annals of Hawksley Manor.'

'Bugger toasting it in coffee!' Ben sprang to his feet and made purposely towards the cellar door. 'This has to be celebrated with a bottle of the Manor's finest!'

'Give us indigestion at this hour,' protested Mrs Buckley, but Eli, his weather beaten face wreathed in a huge grin, slammed his fist on the table making the china dance.

'But bugger than an' all,' he roared, '…make it a couple of bottles, lad, while you're at it!'

'Lord,' Mrs Buckley shook her head. 'You sound just like your old pa I'll be darned if you don't!'

Sophie had a restless night and was wide awake well before daylight. For a long time she lay watching a pale dawn creep across the leaded casement window. In the winter Ben always left the shutters folded back; total darkness, he said, made him feel he was sleeping in a tomb. Sophie propped herself on one elbow and gazed down at him where he lay beside her: in the faint light she could see his tousled dark head and the outlines of that ever-young face against the pillow; imagine the half-smile his mouth always seemed to have as he slept...a great surge of love rose in her and it was with difficulty that she held back from leaning to kiss and wake him for the pure sensual pleasure of having him turn, bury his head in her breast and wrap her in his arms with a sleepy..."Umm...more...more!" Then, of course the familiar dance would begin, no less enjoyable for being so familiar. Each knew the other's body as well as their own and how to give and receive pleasure...

With a sigh she lay back against her own pillows, too troubled about the coming talk she must initiate with her father to even console herself with lovemaking. It would not, she knew by experience, be easy. Over the years since she had reached adulthood they had clashed many times. Although she loved and was fiercely protective of him, and he of her, never-the-less they were like the two sides of an old penny: the King, supreme monarch on one side, Britannia, warlike with her shield and helmet and ready to do battle on the other. More than once during one of their verbal duels he had exploded with an exasperated: "By God, but you remind me of–" then stopped abruptly and ended the exchange by waving a dismissive hand and turning away. One of their more prolonged differences of opinion had been over the twins schooling; Geoffrey expecting them to follow tradition and go away to prep-school at eight, and Sophie having none of it.

"We don't want our children to spend half their childhood away from home," she had said firmly.

"All boys needed the discipline of boarding school...it teaches them to be men," countered her father.

"Well our sons will become men within the family, not out of it,' she'd retorted, "and they'll go to local schools and make friends they can see all year round...quite apart from anything else we simply couldn't afford the fees for Oundle or Sherborne or others of that ilk. We have a good village school and if they are bright enough to pass the entrance exam they can follow in Ben's footsteps and go on to their local grammar school."

"Well thanks to a government who no longer funds them unless they can get a scholarship you'll still have fees to pay, won't you?"

"Very modest ones in comparison for what you shelled out for Rupert and me." Sophie strove to keep her words reasonable, because she *did* understand how hard it was for someone of her father's background and conventional upbringing to accept that times were changing and they must change with them; that sending one's children away to school for others to be *in loco parentis* for eight years was not always the best thing from any point of view. "It isn't just the money, dad, she went on more gently, "and it isn't that I don't appreciate the education you gave us, but I know Rupert wasn't happy to be away from home…to miss all those years of growing up with mother and you…he hated going back, every single time, and so did I."

But her father either couldn't, or wouldn't see her point of view and the argument had continued to rumble on for weeks, but both Sophie and Ben had stood firm and eventually Geoffrey, realising he was fighting a losing battle, had given up and the subject had remained closed.

Ben once asked his wife who else in the family besides her might have been that obstinate and determined in the face of opposition, and she had laughed and answered not her mother for sure, nor her grandmother. But she had often pondered just how much Geoffrey might have gleaned from her mother about the character of Sophie's natural father, and if her determination to overcome any obstacles set in her path, not to mention on occasions her sheer bloody-mindedness, might have been bequeathed her by that long dead Captain Pop, who may, or may not have fathered her…

Sophie drew a deep breath and willed herself to put those old tantalizing thoughts aside; she wouldn't let herself dwell on the past: today must be all about the future.

I will be diplomatic, she vowed, *I will be calm and practical, even if I have to sit and silently burst a blood vessel at all the grief dad is going to give me…*she gave an audible chuckle that made Ben stir in his sleep…*because I know that in the end I'll win!*

* * *

Despite her resolutions she was reluctant to make the short journey to Stable Cottage that morning. Perhaps it was lack of sleep as much as the certain knowledge that presenting Geoffrey with the proposed changes to life at Hawksley would be both fraught and painful that made her find one task after another to delay the meeting. True, she was tired and somewhat hung-over from the previous night's perhaps premature celebrations, but that couldn't account for her uneasy feeling that quite apart from the coming confrontation, something quite different and unpleasant was about to happen.

"Perhaps I'm just depressed," she said aloud as she watched Ben leave in the Land Rover with the boys. It was the first day of school after the Christmas holidays and she had been glad of the distractions of the usual hunt for missing plimsolls and football boots and books before they were finally on their way, hanging from the windows and waving frantically as the Land Rover sped down the drive. She turned into the house, examining the thought: no, it couldn't be that; she never had time to be depressed, so what was it that she felt sitting on her shoulder like Churchill's 'Black Dog'?

When Ben returned from the village he went as usual to check on the vines…"Just in case them'ud walked off in the night," as Tom had once commented. In his absence she made the beds, tidied both Xanda's and Jamies's rooms, rooted out all the grubby socks, pants, shirts and sweaters from corners and under beds and dumped them in the laundry for Mary Hoskins to deal with later when she came up from the village to help clean. After all this she brushed Mavis the cat, who didn't want to be brushed, swept the breakfast crumbs from beneath the boy's chairs then took down the jar of coffee beans and set the old but still functional grinder going ready for Ben's return to the house. They would, she thought, need a good hit of caffeine as well as a united front when they broke their news to her father and Pru.

She heard the side door open as she was pouring water onto the freshly ground coffee and as she did so the telephone in the lobby rang. The door slammed, Ben shouted 'I'll get it,' Sophie called: 'Coffee's ready when you're done,' and set the pot on the stove. She glanced at the clock: almost ten thirty; did that clock always tick so loudly or if it was just that the house seemed extraordinarily quiet for this time on a weekday morning? Mrs Buckley must be feeding the chickens – *they* seemed to have shut down on production for the past few weeks and were busy eating their heads off with very little result. Eli kept threatening to wring a neck or two for the pot and Sophie smiled, remembering how Ben wouldn't let him, because he said, they deserved a few weeks rest after spending months in what for a hen must be a permanent state of pregnancy.

Suddenly Ben was pounding along the passageway and bursting through the kitchen door. For a moment he stood on the threshold, as breathless as though he had run a mile rather than a few yards. 'Sophie…' his voice was hoarse. 'That was Pru – your father's had a bad fall – she's sent for an ambulance…' he grabbed her hand as she started towards him and together they ran; out of the door and down the long pathway Geoffrey had laid over thirty years before to connect the manor with Stable Cottage. Since he and Pru had moved to the cottage after his daughter's wedding he had, up until a handful of years ago, struggled along this path on his crutches, or wheeled himself in his chair every morning to drink his morning coffee in the manor kitchen. Advancing age and failing strength had meant he only made the journey occasionally in his chair and with Pru in attendance, now Ben and Sophie raced down that path he had travelled so often as though the very hounds of hell were at their heels.

* * *

A white-faced Pru was kneeling beside Geoffrey where he lay with closed eyes on the living room floor, his breathing slow and laboured; Sophie's first feeling of relief that there was no sign of blood or any obvious injury was swiftly followed by shock when she knelt to take her father's hand and saw for the first time the swelling on the side of his head; a swelling that seemed to grow beneath her horrified gaze.

Ben crouched to put an arm about Pru. 'What happened?' he asked, 'how long has he been like this?'

'I don't know,' she was distraught. 'I'd been upstairs for at least half an hour making the bed and tidying; I found him when I came down to see if he wanted to go up to the house...he must have fallen and hit his head.' She started to weep. 'It was such a lovely morning...I thought he'd enjoy having his coffee with you...'

Been looked up and at the expression in his eyes Sophie felt the tears welling in her own. *And we were about to come here and spoil it all...half an hour...* she almost wrung her hands in despair...*while I was being a coward and procrastinating he may have been lying unconscious for all that time; we could have been here; we could have helped him.*

Pru was making a heroic effort to be calm. 'As soon as I found him I called the ambulance, then I rang you...I wanted to put a cushion under his head, but I didn't know...'

Her words trailed away. Ben gave Sophie another glance and began to raise Pru to her feet, as he did so the distinctive tone of an ambulance bell sounded in the lane behind the cottage and within minutes the room seemed to be full of people, the three of them hustled to one side as ambulance men brought in a stretcher and a doctor briefly examined the unconscious Geoffrey before directing the men to place him – "Carefully, for God's sake" – on a stretcher – and then they were gone, the urgent ringing of the bell fading away into the distance.

Ben raced back to the house to fetch the Land Rover. Driving to the hospital in a kind of controlled frenzy he covered the distance so quickly that they arrived only minutes behind the ambulance and in time to see Geoffrey, surrounded by nursing staff, being rushed on a trolley from Casualty towards the X-ray department.

The three of them sat on plastic-covered chairs in an overly bright room and waited, it seemed for hours. Pru still wept spasmodically; silently, the tears sliding down her lined face, while Ben sat beside her, a comforting arm about her shoulders. Sophie was numb; dry-eyed, too stunned by the suddenness of it all to weep; too filled with guilt that she hadn't been *there* when he fell: to lift him, to get help more quickly...

At the sound of the opening door they all looked up. The surgeon stood in the doorway, still in theatre greens, mask limp around his neck. He looked from one to the other, eyes full of sympathy and regret. 'I'm sorry, Mrs de Lacy,' he moved further into the room; taking Pru's hand gently between his own he said, 'your husband had an abnormally thin skull and the fracture he sustained when he fell caused a massive bleed into the brain. There was nothing we could do.'

Sophie sat frozen, unable at first to grasp the finality of his words. *This isn't real,* she thought, *no one should go like that...just snuffed out in minutes...*abruptly she stood and walked to the window staring out at the cold, crisp morning where a pale winter sun turned the frosty grass before the hospital into a sparkling carpet of tiny diamond drops.

*Oh, dad...you fought a war and survived...and you were so strong. I remember before the accident how you rode hard and hunted and fished...and all that's been snuffed out because you wouldn't give in and wait for Pru to help you – you just had to go it alone, didn't you...*she gave a strangled gulp; half sob, half laughter; *you probably tripped over your own feet and fell, you stubborn old devil...*

With a tremendous effort of will she wrenched her mind back to the reality of the moment: she might let herself go to pieces later, but not now; not here in this anonymous room, in front of this tired man in his bizarre garments. Pru needed her; when they came home from school the boys would need her...with steely resolve she kept her tears at bay; moving to the weeping Pru's side she knelt and wrapped her arms around her.

'Pru dear, there is nothing more we can do here. Come home with us and rest and afterward we can talk about what must be done.' She

76

raised questioning eyes to the surgeon; 'Perhaps come back later and say goodbye?'

He nodded, relieved. 'Yes…by all means…later this afternoon.'

Docile now and exhausted, Geoffrey de Lacy's widow allowed them to lead her back to the Land Rover and the long sad journey back to Hawksley.

They buried him alongside his mother, wife and son, in Hawksley churchyard beneath the shade of the ancient yews. Before that year ended Pru lay beside them; victim of an inoperative, invasive cancer that had probably, the doctor said, been hastened by the shock of Geoffrey's death.

In the spring of the following year, when Sophie laid sheaves of the first of the bright yellow daffodils from the Manor grounds on each of the five graves, she thought about all the years she had carried out this same simple task: first for her mother, Rupert and her grandmother; then for her father; now for her dear, loving and much loved Pru, who had come into their lives after Claire and Rupert's deaths and made her own and her father's shattered and fragmented lives whole again. Now there was no member of her Hawksley family left; no one with whom to talk over old times; to ask: "do you remember when?"

She could only hope and pray that this year would be a better, less stressful one than the last. Nineteen seventy-five, with all the fighting and civil wars across the globe; a devastating hurricane in America; starvation in Bangladesh and dodgy politics at home had brought little joy in the wider sense and a great deal of grief and heartache to her own small corner of the world.

It was some comfort to remember that Pru had unexpectedly approved the plans for the Manor and at the united urging of Ben, the twins, and Sophie herself, had moved after Geoffrey's funeral back into the main house, where she had taken a keen interest in the comings and goings of all the workmen who invaded the West wing from the end of January through to April, when Hawksley opened its doors once again to the first visitors of the season. It was almost as though the changes taking place around her had come as a welcome relief; some kind of antidote to her sudden loss and she remained interested and alert until her death, which came with merciful swiftness as the year drew to an end.

Jamie and Xander missed their grandparents terribly; Geoffrey and Pru had been an important part of their young lives and Stable

Cottage a second home. There they could play the endless board games that sent Sophie crazy but both grandparents were happy to play for hours. In the months following Pru's death Ben took the boys on Saturdays in term time and more frequently in school holidays to Kidlington, where his own parents welcomed the chance to spoil their grandchildren; when they returned in the evening from these outings Julius would often come with them as a welcome guest. Now well into his eighties he was perhaps the one person who appeared timeless; who never seemed to alter, but stood steady as an ancient rock amid the swirling tides of change that patterned their lives.

* * *

To Sophie and Ben's great relief none of their visitors that year appeared to mind, or comment adversely on the only partially muted sounds of workman still busy on the East wing, nor of the slightly reduced tour of the house itself; seeming content with the improved decoration and furnishing of those rooms remaining on view: the popular tearooms – which now had the extra attraction of the Manor's own bottles of sparkling white wine for sale – and the immaculate grounds, recently mightily upgraded, proved an even greater attraction than before due to the combined efforts of Tom, Eli and a couple of students from the nearby Agricultural College willing to sacrifice their spare time and vacations to add extra cash to their grants.

Through all the planning, the upheaval of the entire household, the brick and plaster dust that invaded every corner of the old house; the sawing and banging and shouting, the endless cups of tea; the plastering, the painting, the swearing, the laughter, Sophie moved: checking, encouraging, issuing orders, soothing fraying tempers; holding the whole exercise firmly together in her capable hands, and Ben watched her, marvelling at the total commitment she gave to the regeneration of her home while still managing always to *be* there – for the failing Pru and her dearest Bucky; for Jamie and Alexander, and most of all, for Ben himself. Tired, sometimes, irritable and stressed at the end of one of those particularly hectic days when just everything seemed to go wrong, late in the evening she would still be at work: papers, plans, accounts paid and bills to be paid strewn across the kitchen table. Coffee mug in one hand, the other pushed up into that shining head of hair, when the old wall clock struck midnight she would wave a celebratory coffee mug and announce: "Cheers – tighten your seatbelts, folks... here comes another day!"

No wonder he loved her so much.

CHAPTER 10

Hawksley, April 1976

Easter; the newly created, carpeted and decorated apartments in the West wing lacked only the finishing touch of curtains to make them ready for viewing and on the first morning of Jamie and Alexander's school holidays Sophie took them with her up to the old servant's quarters at the top of the house, ostensibly to help her sort through the mixture of useless junk and near priceless items for any such window furnishings that might be suitable.

Of course, she might have known that one of the first things they would discover and fall upon with whoops of joy was the large wooden chest filled with the carefully packed and stored childhood memorabilia from Rupert's old room, long since turned into the office she and Ben now shared. She stopped her own unpacking of a cabin trunk filled with curtaining to watch them exclaim and enthuse over the old farm animals and buildings, the dog eared books: *Billy Bunter, Just William, Biggles* and *The Saint;* the delicate balsa wood 'planes and aircraft magazines, the latter pounced on by Jamie with howls of delight – and at first cast aside before catching the attention of Alexander who retrieved it from the floor where it had been dropped, a thick octavo book, the red cloth cover fading and rubbed: Rupert's Picture Album.

'Bags I the 'planes and mags.' Jamie was already pouring over the magazines while his twin, abandoning the farm animals he had begun to place in a neat pile beside the trunk, sat cross-legged, the album balanced on his grubby knees. Stroking a finger over the cover he read aloud: 'This photograph album belongs to Rupert Hamilton de Lacy, Hawksley Manor, Hampshire, England, The World, The Universe, Outer Space…Gosh, mum,' he turned shining eyes toward Sophie, 'look at this…may I have it; may I?'

For a moment Sophie sat still, her own eyes fixed on her son's eager face before giving a rueful smile. *Oh well, it had to happen sometime…*she said, 'Yes, but be very careful with it; keep it in your own room.'

Both boys knew, in a vague, small boy way, that there had been an uncle and a grandma, killed in an accident long before they were born and that same accident was why grandpa had always walked with sticks and sometimes had to use a wheelchair. Knew also in the same distant way that Geoffrey wasn't really their mother's father, nor Pru her mother, but were still of an age where the finer intricacies of family relationships had not yet slotted into place and had as yet been of much interest to either boy. But now, seeing her son's face alight with excitement and curiosity, Sophie knew that when he looked through Rupert's album, he would, as she had done twenty years before, wonder who the tall American was and why he had been such an important person in their uncle's life.

She continued to lift the sets of curtains; shaking them and holding them to the light to make sure they were whole and undamaged, all the time keeping half an eye on Alexander, where he still sat pouring over the open book. First he turned every page to the end, then repeated the manoeuvre; then turned back again to a page almost at the end; to the picture of her mother and the tall American by the five-barred gate into Belstead wood. This he studied for a minute or two then looked up, his face solemn. 'This is your real daddy, isn't it?' he asked.

Sophie drew a sharp breath and actually felt it whistle though her lungs as she let it escape. She said huskily, 'What makes you say that?'

He answered simply, 'Because you look just like him.'

'He might be, Xanda. I can't be sure,' she kept her tone neutral.

'How can't you be sure?' Jamie, ever practical chipped in. He came over to squat beside his twin. 'How can't you?'

She said baldy, honestly, 'Because he was killed in the war before I was born...and because no-one ever told me.'

Jamie persisted. 'Why didn't they tell you?'

'I don't know...perhaps no one thought there was any point as he was dead.'

There was silence for a moment; Alexander said hesitantly, 'I look like him too, a bit, don't I?'

'Yes.'

'That's because I look like you, I suppose.'

'Well *I* look like dad – and he's still alive,' said Jamie, with brutal honesty.

'Captain Pop's a funny sort of name, isn't it?' Alexander's blue eyes were puzzled. 'I never heard of anyone with a name like that.'

She said, 'I think it was a sort of nickname Rupert had for him.'

Patience was not Jamie's strong point. 'What was his *real* name, then?' he demanded.

With difficulty Sophie held onto her own patience. 'I don't *know.*' This had gone far enough for now. 'Look,' she said reasonably; 'we have to leave it there for now...I must get these curtains sorted. Why don't you each find an empty box and take the things you'd like to keep to your own rooms?'

With relief she watched them leave with their booty in separate cardboard boxes. Mechanically, she went on sorting through the curtains. It had been a long time since she'd really thought about her natural father. Although Geoffrey's death had stirred old thoughts and emotions, out of loyalty to him she had pushed them to one side; now, thanks to her sons persistent questioning they were back with a vengeance. She looked across the attic to Rupert's trunk that held so many memories; surely even at this late date, with all her immediate family gone, there must be some way she could find out about the man her mother had loved, who flew off one morning and never came back. She should do that, even if only to help her boys understand.

Not loyal Bucky, she thought; it would distress her; she couldn't do that...but, Tom and Eli? Of course, they'd only been young teenagers then and probably hadn't had much cause to be around the house at the time; still, it was worth a try; they might at least have seen him; heard gossip. However hard the parties concerned might have tried to keep the secret, the presence of a strange American at the manor would surely have caused some speculation amongst the staff. Tomorrow, she decided, when Ben took Jamie and Xanda to Kidlington she'd catch Tom and Eli before they left to go home for their lunch and ask them outright.

* * *

The following morning Sophie caught up with her quarry, hastening down the steps before the house and waving them down just as they were leaving for home.

Tom slowed his old Ford truck, cranked on the handbrake and leaned from the open window. 'Where's the fire, then?' he asked.

'No fire,' Sophie put her hand on the door. 'Are you in a frightful hurry for your lunch, or could you both spare me a few minutes...well, probably a touch more than a few: I need to ask you something.'

The brothers exchanged glances then nodded. Eli said, 'Right-o, but where? There ain't room for three of us in this here cab.'

Sophie stepped up onto the running board and hitched an arm over the open window. 'Bless you; just drive around to the back terrace – we'll use the study. I've left the French windows on the latch.'

'Top secret, eh?' Tom grinned and put the truck into gear. 'It 'ud better be a good 'un cause I'll get a right ear-wiggin' from the missus if I'm late fer me lunch!'

Once inside the study, Sophie made the brothers sit on the worn leather chesterfield, poured three whiskeys, then drew up a chair and seated herself in front of them.

'I want you to tell me what you know about someone who visited the manor during the war; someone my mother knew well: an American airman Rupert called Captain Pop.'

Tom said, 'Bugger all!' and slopped his whisky; Eli said something unrepeatable and took a large gulp at his own drink; both looked, Sophie thought, as though she'd upped and threatened them with a shotgun.

'Sorry about that, Sophie luv,' Eli recovered himself quickly, 'but what the 'ell are you wanting to know about all that stuff – years ago it was an' all forgotten by most folk.'

'Oh, come off it, Eli...just look at me; how could *anyone* forget!' Sophie, now she had taken the plunge was in no mood to prevaricate any longer. 'Look, I *know* he was my father...I just want to know more about him, that's all.'

The brother's exchanged glances; shrugged in unison, nodded and chorused a grudging 'OK,' reminding Sophie that although not twins there was barely a year between them and they appeared to share a silent language and communicate their thoughts in much the same way as her Jamie and Alexander did from time to time.

'See, us'n didn't really know the Captain or 'ave all that much to do with him; only saw him on an' off, like, although he was allus very friendly an' used ter bring us boys sweets – candy, he called it.' Elias rubbed his chin and gave a reminiscent grin. 'I remember first time we saw him he come loggin' with us ...that were when he first come to up to the 'ouse, but we could see right away him and Missus Claire was sweet on each other.'

'After that they was always about together,' put in Tom, 'he used to ride Sampson alongside 'er on her mare Dolly, an' they'd be off to the forest fer most of the day. When Rupert was home from school they'd take picnics to the beach and that sort of thing. Missus Marion – Old Mrs de Lacy, she turned the blindest eye you ever seen to the goings on ...she knowed Mr Geoffrey was allus after other women and wasn't the 'usband he should have been, even before he went off to the war, an' I guess she wanted to see missus Claire happy like for once, even if it couldn't last...I'm sorry, luv, but your ma 'adn't 'ad much of a life until the Captain came.'

Eli nodded sagely. 'Used ter go to Lunnon fer the weekends when 'e had leave they did, and she'd come back blooming like a summer rose.'

'His name,' prompted Sophie, 'please...tell me his name.'

They exchanged another looked; shrugged again. Tom answered her.

'Petersen,' he said, 'Captain Petersen, only he was a Major be the time he was killed.'

'Where was he stationed – what airfield? It must have been nearby.'

'Don't know,' Eli shook his head. 'See, in the war you didn't say and nobody asked. There used to be all them notices pinned up: "Careless Talk Costs Lives" an' "Wall 'ave Ears" an' things like that. Missus must 'ave known, o' course and the old lady; maybe Mrs Buckley. But no one never told us.'

Tom was thoughtful. 'Might 'ave been the one at Stony Cross...or Beaulieu, though that's a bit far...he didn't allus come in one o' them jeep things; sometimes he walked.' He looked at his brother, 'what was that place called where they 'ad them great Flying Fortress things we'd see go over – t'other side of Hawksley village, warn't it – between there and Stafford Lay?' He dug Eli in the ribs. 'Remember Eddie Marsh what was killed on his motor-bike a year or more back? 'Is dad was the pot man at The Bull pub at Stafford Lay in the war an' Eddie always 'ad sweets galore 'cause the Yanks from the airfield used ter drink there.'

Eli scratched his head. 'Sommat to do with a bird, it was... Skylark...Eagle...'

'Falcon!' Tom shouted, and gave his brother's shoulder an almighty whack, 'Falcon Field; that was it!'

Sophie sat back, nursing her glass and feeling quite light-headed. His name had been Petersen and he'd been stationed at somewhere called Falcon Field...again her memory stirred, remembering her bike ride through Belstead Wood with Rupert all those years ago: the deserted airfield; the tower they'd climbed; Rupert's silence as he'd stood staring down the runway. How her legs had ached when they were cycling home and he'd told her it was her own fault for tagging along, and how cross she'd been because he said if she told mummy or daddy where they'd been he wouldn't take her anywhere else again, ever...

'How far is it from here: this Falcon Field?'

Eli hunched his shoulders. 'Don't know; don't even know *where* it is. There was airfields scattered all over the Forest then, but who'd

84

need 'em after the war? It's probably been built over be now... ten years ago a lot of houses went up outside of Stafford Lay.'

'Belstead Wood,' she said aloud, 'could you get to it through Belstead Wood?'

'Search me.' Tom drained his glass and stood up, closely followed by Eli. 'Sorry Sophie, luv...but my missus really will cut up rough if the dinner spoils, an' we've got a powerful lot of work to put in on the lake when we gets back...Jimmy Trent's over wi' the dredger this afternoon an' his time costs money.'

'It's OK. Thanks anyway,' Sophie walked with them down to the truck. 'Do you remember the American's first name?'

'Oh, yeah,' Tom swung into the cab. 'Ryan...sounds Irish don't it? See you later. Missus.'

Sophie watched the truck out of sight before turning back towards the house. *Ryan Petersen*...now why did the name somehow strike a chord? She gave herself a mental shake: with all she had learned today crowding her mind if she wasn't careful she'd begin to imagine all sorts of things.

Ben didn't arrive back with their boys and Julius until the late afternoon. Tom and Eli were busy at the lake, Mrs Buckley had gone to Salisbury to visit her niece and Sophie had the place to herself for most of the day. As usual the house had been open for the Easter weekend, and next week it would start all over again. She had been too busy to iron the curtains she'd taken from the attic but now she settled to her least favourite household chore, stacking each set as she finished ironing them into neat piles in the chosen rooms; later she would get Ben to climb the long ladder and hang them. While she worked she thought about Ryan Petersen, the man her mother had loved so much that she had carried, and kept, his child. Now she had a face and a name for him, and probably the airfield he flew from. None of which made him any less dead and unattainable, but it was a comfort...more than a comfort, rather a putting to bed of a problem; a – what was it the Americans called it? She wracked her brain – "closure"...that was it: she had closure.

Or she would have if she could find Falcon Field again: just to look at it, to think about Ryan Petersen, who had never seen his daughter's face, nor watched his grandsons grow up.

The next morning, after the twins had left the house to help cut back the reeds and watch the lake being dredged, Sophie brought a tray of coffee out to the front terrace where Ben and Julius were already seated, and as unemotionally as she could, told them about her talk with Eli and Tom.

Ben let out his breath softly and hunched forward to take her hand. 'That must have been so hard for you to do,' he said.

She twined her fingers in his, barely holding back sudden tears.

One of Ben's most endearing traits was his utter involvement and interest and support in everything to do with her life. His own family was extended, close and almost complete: grandfather, father, mother, brother, uncles, aunts; a dozen or more cousins, near and far. Sophie knew he felt keenly her own lack of family. All those of her family she had known in childhood were gone; all her future was in him their sons and this house. Only Ben would truly guess how hard it had been; how difficult to step back into her past and for the sake of Jamie and Alexander, whose curiosity about her parentage had been sparked by the discovery of Rupert's album, to practically beg two old friends such as Tom and Eli to break the silence and bring her a step closer to knowing her father.

'My dear,' Julius spoke gently. 'How best can an old man help you?'

She lifted her shoulders. 'I wish I knew. Now that the twins have discovered Rupert's album and made the connection between his Captain pop and me, I can't just leave it there: Xanda is particularly curious and I can see there will be many more questions coming my way very soon.'

Julius was silent for a few moments, then said thoughtfully, 'is there perhaps one picture in that album which says all you feel about you father? Something that would help you explain more about him to them?'

'Yes,' Sophie's reply was prompt, almost without thought. 'There is one of him and my mother at the old wooden five barred gate at the far side of the vineyard...the one we had to replace a few years back when it finally gave in to the years, I've always felt there was something special about that picture.' She wrinkled her brow. 'I have a feeling it could have been a regular meeting place...you see, if my mother was a Red Cross VAD at the local cottage hospital, she would have walked to it along the lane that runs between our land and Belstead wood – it would have been a short cut; much better than going by road, because petrol was rationed and she'd have been unlikely to have used the car. Also, if she and my father sometimes wanted to meet away from prying eyes, *he* might have walked through the wood from this Falcon Field to meet her. Tom said he often came on foot and I'm sure that must have been the airfield Rupert and I cycled to through the wood that time.' She smiled at Julius. 'It is a lovely picture…the way they are looking at each other: it says it all without words.'

'Then you should perhaps have it made a bigger copy and put in a frame…place it where everyone can see; then he will not be dead and forgotten, but a good memory to keep alive… a proof and reminder of his love for your mother.'

Ben saw and guessed her hesitation. He said, 'It wouldn't be disloyal to Geoffrey, darling; *he'll* always be the dad you loved and who loved you. I know he found it impossible to talk about the past when he was alive but I'm sure, given the close relationship he had with his own grandchildren, he wouldn't now begrudge Jamie and Xanda knowing about their *other* grandfather.'

So that was what she did and when the picture was framed and stood in the drawing room for all to see, the questions came thick and fast and she answered them, feeling as she did so a great surge of relief. Now her past was out in the open, as wise old Julius had said "for all to see". She was the daughter of Claire de Lacy and Captain Ryan Petersen, who had loved and lost each other over thirty years ago.

Alexander and Jamie were delighted by the revelation that they had a previously unknown grandfather, one moreover who had been a wartime hero; a bomber pilot and American to boot. None of their friends had such a glamorous being in their past. Jamie in particular, who after a visit to the Farnham Air Show when he was five had announced that he was going to fly an airplane when he grew up, was excited beyond measure that he had a grandfather who had actually piloted a Flying Fortress…

On hearing this Sophie had muttered at the time: "Over my dead body you'll ever fly a plane!" while Ben had commented that perhaps there was more to nature than to nurture, and that inherited genes might in time prove to be more powerful than one might think.

CHAPTER 11

Hawksley, July 1976

By the beginning of July that year work on the house was complete, all the apartments tenanted and Sophie had added to her work load the task of discreetly overseeing the clutch of strangers, who in the fullness of time would stay, many of them to become close friends. So far the whole enterprise had gone almost without a hitch. Almost...but there was always one, Sophie found, the proverbial Fly in the Ointment; the Square Peg that wouldn't fit into the Round Hole in the person of Major General Fforbes-Pomfrey, who had been a prime example of that genre. Outraged that *children* were actually allowed within shouting distance of the Manor he had departed in high dudgeon after only a month in his luxury apartment, his place swiftly filled by Jane and Paul Webster, who having brought up four children of their own had no such phobia about the young.

But the past year had been a punishing schedule of almost unremitting hard work with the house and grounds open as usual to the paying public, the drive to finish all the apartments on time; selecting would-be tenants from a surprisingly long list of applicants sent to view by the Ringwood Estate Agents; the settling in of same tenants and the resulting interminable office work this all entailed left Sophie little time for leisure. Ben too had worked from dawn to dusk in the vineyard and the myriad tasks associated with it, most notably the regular spraying of the vines against mildew – an exhausting job of hand spraying every plant whilst carrying a cumbersome backpack of chemicals; a task that would have taken him four or five days of backbreaking toil had Tom and Eli not taken some of the burden from his aching shoulders. Even with their willing help the task had left even the indomitably cheerful Ben wilting under the pressure.

It was during this time of stress that Sophie felt more than grateful for the equable and cheerful nature of the twins, who after an early childhood devoted to a degree of naughtiness that had to be experienced to be believed, had begun showing an increasing ability to keep occupied and reasonably out of mischief during those hours not spent in school or sleep.

Although Jamie had only a passing interest in and little aptitude for actually working in the great outdoors, preferring to spend his leisure hours at the kitchen table building model aircraft and racing cars from kits purchased with his weekly pocket money; in contrast, Alexander was almost always to be found in the vineyard with his father, or working alongside Tom and Eli in the greenhouse, orchard or vegetable garden, all of which had grown under the brother's expert care and now supplied the manor, their own families and most of the tenants with fresh fruit and vegetables all year round. With their own chickens for eggs and the pot along with any hare, rabbit or pheasant shot on the estate, milk, butter, lamb and beef from Pete Morgan at Home Farm...and of course, no shortage of wine to accompany the evening meal, almost without noticing, Hawksley had become practically self-sufficient;.

Sometimes Sophie found the days and weeks passed too swiftly; there was so much to do; so little time to sit back and enjoy all they had achieved. Soon enough their sons would move from the comfortable small world of the village school into the larger world of Bramstead Grammar; instead of the short drive to school each morning there would be a longer one to the station and the train that would take them even further from home.

Where had the past years gone, never mind about the weeks – and when had she and Ben settled into this cosy, loving, but no longer quite such exciting relationship? They still made love and enjoyed it, but certainly less often. They went out to dinner with friends, entertained at Hawksley from time to time, but how long had it been since they went up to the West End as they used to in the early days of their marriage? When did they ever see a play or attend a concert anywhere more exciting or far flung than the village hall, or at a pinch, Bournemouth?

God, she thought, closing the vineyard account book and slumping back in her chair, could total stagnation be far off?

But looking on the bright side, and there *was* a bright side despite the pressures of work, they still managed to snatch a week or two each summer in France, while for the past four years Christmas through to New Year had been enlivened by all four de la Tour' s staying *en famille* at Hawksley. For Sophie, who loved entertaining at any time and especially at Christmas, the presence at the Manor of Caro and Charles, Hélène and Dominic was something to look forward to in the depths of a Hampshire winter...here she automatically suppressed the treacherous little jump of pleasure around the region of her ribcage that the mere thought of Dominic could still arouse, even after all these years.

She sighed, picked up her pencil and began to doodle whorls and spirals and things that might be daisies on the back of a paid account.

I'm married, have a loving husband and two super sons; I have good friends, sufficient money, security and a lovely home. I do not need Dominic de la Tour to make my life complete...

'Penny for them', said Ben, coming up behind her and resting his hands on her shoulders.

She turned smiling to lay a hand over one of his. 'Not even worth that,' she said, and that was true, more or less.

* * *

September, 1977

Just before the end of the summer holidays and when the boys were due to begin at the Grammar School the following week, the Nicholls household was increased by two additional members: a pair of large, long legged un-coordinated black Labrador puppies rejoicing in the names of Starsky and Hutch, a gift from Pete Morgan at Home Farm when his Labrador Megan excelled herself by producing a litter of twelve.

The twins were delighted... 'Just like Uncle Rupert's Gunner,' crooned Alexander, cradling a squirming black Starsky in his arms and letting it wash his face with a hot pink tongue, while his twin rolled on the floor with Hutch who bypassing the face washing, growled ferociously and tugged at Jamie's sweater.

Sophie regarded the two new additions with mixed feelings. It would be lovely to have a dog about the place again; that had been impossible while Mildred, the last of the cats reigned over the manor, but since she had passed to the happy hunting grounds a year ago the place had definitely lacked a four-footed presence...but *eight* feet... wasn't that going a touch too far? But she simply hadn't the heart to refuse Pete when he'd appeared in the manor kitchen that morning, a wriggling bundle under each arm.

'I couldn't pass these last two onto just anyone,' he said. 'All the others have gone as gundogs, but these fellas,' he'd glanced ruefully from one to the other. 'Dunno what went wrong there, but they both jump outta their skins even when my lad fires his airgun!'

'How old are they?' Sophie eyed the pair dubiously.

'Going on fifteen weeks...should have been long gone be now.'

She raised a sceptical eyebrow. 'House trained?'

Pete said cautiously, 'Sort of!'

She sighed. 'That's what I thought.'

Ben had grinned at the new family members when he came in for lunch. 'Just in time for the boys to leave for school earlier, come back later and duck out of most of the work...I can take a guess at who'll be doing the feeding, walking and house training,' and he cocked a meaningful eyebrow at Sophie.

Jamie asked: 'What's house training?' just as Hutch did an impressive puddle on the kitchen floor.

'This is,' Sophie threw him an old towel. 'Now tell him he's a bad boy, mop that up, take him outside and stay with him until he does another of those. *Then* you can make a fuss of him, tell him he's a good boy and fetch him back in...And as for you, Xanda,' she pointed at son number two, 'take Starsky out and do the same with him before we have another happening.'

She watched them go and gave the grinning Ben a long look.

'In answer to your comment, *everyone* – and that includes the lord and master – will participate in feeding, walking grooming *and* house training. Consistency and patience are the keys to success.'

'Blimey,' said Ben. 'D'you think Pete would mind if we gave them back?'

Of course they stayed and of course Sophie was the prime carer, walker, feeder and toilet trainer, but she had to admit Starsky and Hutch certainly brought a new, brighter dimension to all their lives. For her in particular they provided the perfect excuse to regularly put aside all other work and walk; just walk, as she hadn't made time to do for years. Every morning when the immediate household tasks were completed she donned good walking shoes, an old Barbour and set off along the numerous footpaths and lanes that bisected the countryside around Hawksley, the two puppies at first straining at the leash, but soon running free and gambolling around her heels like young lambs in springtime.

It was in the midst of all this blooming of family life that tragedy struck again.

CHAPTER 12

Hampshire, July 1978

They were in France with Charles and Caroline when the news came about Julius. Ben pulled every string available to fly home on the same day, leaving Sophie to transfer the remaining 'plane tickets for herself and their boys to the next available flight. At the height of the tourist season it was almost forty-eight hours before their forlorn and depleted little party arrived back at Hawksley. With a distressed and tearful Jamie and Alexander to care for and comfort, Sophie had little time for her own grief and although she needed desperately to be with Ben and his family she had to put her own needs on hold until she had settled their son's into their own familiar surroundings for the night. Sophie, who knew all too well the agony of loss, felt their pain and bewilderment as though it were her own, but knew how little even she could do to make their childish world come the right way up again. Only time and the happy memories they had of Julius would help them fill the void his passing had left.

That night Jamie and Alexander slept in a guest room, where they could have the comfort of being together and she sat between the twin beds until they were asleep. When she left them at last, first propping open the door with a stuffed toy and leaving a light on in the passage-way, she went slowly down to the ever welcoming kitchen and Bucky's open arms.

'I'm sorry this is such a sad homecoming,' she said, returning the old lady's hug, clinging for a moment as she had as a child. 'Ben said the funeral would be tomorrow so we will have to leave early. Although the family are not orthodox, there will be a Rabbi to say the prayers – Ben was rather wondering where they'd find one of those in deepest Oxfordshire.' She sat at the table, accepting the inevitable cup of tea set before her and gave a little smile. 'Apparently a Jewish funeral is a very low key affair without anything like our church service and hymns; only the men folk go to it, the women stay at home.'

'Well I never,' Mrs Buckley was scandalized; 'you'll be telling me next they don't even have a proper cold collation afterward!'

'I don't know about that, but with the family being unorthodox and rather mixed up with bishops and what-not I shouldn't think it will be all that different. Actually I think it sounds rather more civilised than our trappings of weeping females, dreary hymns and the vicar droning on for hours.' Sophie couldn't resist teasing dear old Bucky a little. 'It's a wonder we don't still have hired mutes walking in front of the coffin.'

'Well, I'm sure I'll feel more comfortable and settled with all my folk, male and female, around me when I make my last journey,' she answered firmly and Sophie had to stifle a smile at the thought of Bucky supervising her own funeral.

But later as she climbed into the bed which seemed so large and empty without Ben she wept again for the loss of Julius; that gentle, mischievous, generous, clever old friend, and knew that for all those who had known and loved him the world would be a sadder and emptier place.

* * *

She left early the following day to make the journey to Kidlington; a subdued Alexander and Jamie side-by-side in the back of the Rover. They had asked to go and Ben had agreed that at almost twelve they were old enough to join him and the rest of the men in laying Papa Julian to rest. In their grey flannel suits, grey shirts and black ties Sophie thought they looked like a pair of rather odd and elderly children. She didn't know quite what to expect of the gathering that awaited them but guessed that like them, most of the mourners would be strangers to this unfamiliar ritual of death.

Her heart ached for Sarah, excluded from following her father on his last journey; apart from a couple of elderly distant cousins there was no one from her side of the family left to support her, and certainly no one close to lean on, so she would need both daughters-in-law by her side for what would be a sad and weary day.

Rather Ben than me having to go through it all at the graveside, Sophie thought, and wondered if the august Bishop uncle would be there with his flamboyant purple vest and conspicuous gold cross... would he too be required to wear a *yarmulke*? Then she gave up worrying about anyone's religious feelings being trampled upon and concentrated on the road ahead.

Her sense of direction was practically non-existent and she was famous for going at least twice and sometimes even more times, around each roundabout she came to before taking the plunge onto what she hoped was the right road for her destination. The twins had always found this manoeuvre excruciatingly funny and would howl with laughter as she drove round and around peering anxiously at the road signs, but today they stayed silent only exchanging a faint, complicit grin at each circuit.

They arrived at Kidlington barely an hour before the men left for the cemetery, which was a good half-hour drive away. Sophie had explained to the twins that they would have to wear the *yarmulke* and warned them not to either giggle or protest when the time came to have theirs fixed in place with *kipah* clips; these looked so like the metal devices used by hairdressers to set their clients curls in place that she felt she had to pre-empt any unseemly response from either son at what must be a solemn moment.

It was cowardly, she knew, as Ben was almost as ignorant as she was about all the niceties of the occasion and was relying heavily on one of the ancient cousins to get himself, his father and brother Guy through the day, but she couldn't wait to turn both boys over to him and concentrate her attention on Sarah, who was much calmer and composed than she'd expected.

After the men had left, Guy's wife, Geraldine, always the busy practical one and not much into hand-holding and bending a sympathetic ear, swept her somewhat rebellious sixteen year old daughter Linda into the kitchen to plate the vast amount of food she had brought with her, although Sarah had gently insisted on making for the more orthodox elderly cousins some traditional egg dishes, which were already arranged and in the larder covered with cling film.

'Papa went so peacefully,' she told Sophie, as they sat in the drawing room over glasses of Russian tea, Sarah's favourite beverage, 'in the evening he just said he felt tired and went early to bed, then next morning I took his breakfast...' she stopped momentarily to press a handkerchief to her eyes, 'but when I put the tray down he shook his head. He said: "I think it is time, my darling" – then just closed his eyes and that was that. He never spoke again but died just an hour or so later.' She smiled through her tears and clasped Sophie's hand. 'He had a good, long life with his family about him – and he would be so pleased to know that Jamie and Alexander are here to say goodbye; it will all seem strange to them but for a Jew the service is short – just prayers and some readings at the graveside and each must put their shovels of earth on the coffin, then it is over.' She smiled again. 'We shall not keep *Shiva* – I wouldn't know how! – but remember him as he was and keep him always in our thoughts.'

And so the day was one of quiet remembrance amid the family and Julius's many friends. In the late evening, when all the other guests had left, Sarah bade her younger son and his family goodbye. Standing in the lighted doorway, Hugh's arm around her, she looked so beautiful and serene that Sophie felt tears start to her eyes.

'She will be all right, won't she?' she asked Ben as they turned into the winding country lane that would take them to the main road and the A40 to begin the long journey home. 'I said we could stay but she insisted the boys would need to sleep in their own familiar beds tonight.'

'She'll be OK...all she really needs now is dad, and he always comes up trumps...he may be quiet and a bit of a stick-in the-mud, but he loves her very much and there's nobody better to take care of her now.'

'There were no hymns,' commented Xanda from the back seat, 'Just prayers and things...and all in Hebrew. It was OK though 'cause we didn't have to hang around long. I think Papa Julius would have like that – he always liked to get on with things, didn't he, mum.'

'He certainly did,' she agreed.

'*I* liked it,' said Jamie, 'apart from those hat things...I thought they were a bit girlie, but the food was good.'

'And there goes any likely conversion to Judaism,' said Ben, *sotto voce.*

Sophie laughed, her spirits lightening. 'Julius would have liked to know they enjoyed the food, seeing that he could always clear his own plate, whatever it contained,' she said.

Xanda leaned forward. 'Mum, can you make some of that egg stuff grandma cooked?'

'Oh, sure she can,' Ben turned his head briefly and gave her a wink, 'she'll do fish balls and gefelterfish too if you ask her nicely.'

Xanda wrinkled his nose. 'Just the egg stuff will do,' he said.

Sophie rested her head against Ben's shoulder. Yes, she thought, Julius would have enjoyed the whole day, and felt the tears begin to slide down her cheeks again at the remembrance of his warmth and wisdom; his sly humour and how he could tease without hurt or malice.

So many people she had lost, all very dear to her, but somehow she knew she would miss Papa Julius most of all.

CHAPTER 13

Hampshire November 1979

On impulse, one sparkling November morning Sophie buttered a couple of scones, put them with a hunk of cheese into a Tupperware box and filled a thermos with coffee. Mrs Buckley watched in silence as Sophie packed both items into an old haversack and when she could contain her curiosity no longer demanded, 'Whatever are you doing? I didn't think things were so bad that you'd be leaving home!'

Sophie laughed. 'I feel like a really long walk today,' she said, 'I don't know when I'll be back so I'm taking my lunch with me. Come along, chaps,' she opened the kitchen door for Hutch and Starsky, 'this morning we're going for what might be quite some hike through the woods.'

Skirting the vineyard she went through the iron five-bared gate at the end of the big meadow and crossing the narrow lane beyond began walking along the ride through Belstead Wood.

It was a longer walk than she'd thought, and much, much further than she remembered. After what had to have been a mile she stopped to sit on a fallen tree for a short rest. How on earth had her six year-old legs peddled so far she wondered? Surely she must be almost through to the far side by now, but it was a further ten minutes before she left the shelter of the trees. Stepped out from the woodland onto another narrow lane she was confronted by the beginning of open heath land and a signpost, one arm pointing right towards Stafford Lay and Brockenhurst, the other left towards Burley.

For a full minute she stood hesitating. The long walk along the sometimes twisting path the broad ride had become during her passage through the wood had made her lose all sense of direction; even worse, she had absolutely no recollection of which way Rupert might have led her after this point, but Eli had said there'd been an airfield on the Stafford Ley side of Hawksley so it seemed reasonable to begin walking towards the village. There was always a chance someone would remember where the legendary B17s had been based.

'Come on, boys,' she stood up, dusting the lichen from the fallen tree from her tweed skirt, 'let's press on towards Stafford Ley and see if we can find out something more about this Falcon Field.'

She had often driven through the village but never actually had reason to stop to visit either the one general stores-come-post office, or it's only other attraction, the Bull Inn. Although the shop appeared open, even at eleven in the morning the street was empty of any human life and the few cottages dotted around the small green might have been deserted for all she could see; only a large and overfed tabby cat lay on a wall before a glaringly new bungalow, the windows hung with strangely dated heavy lace curtains. The cat yawned as the dogs skittered past;

Sophie said 'Hello cat,' and it blinked an insolent yellow eye at her before commencing to nonchalantly wash its nether regions.

The inn was at the far end of the short street; very rustic and picture-postcard, with a thatched roof and long wooden benches either side of the heavy oak door. The inn sign hung slightly crooked and an ancient plane tree stood on a small area of grass before the narrow forecourt. As she approached a couple of old men emerged from a narrow path alongside the building to take up residence on one of the benches, simultaneously producing pipes and tobacco tins preparatory to settling down for a good lung-clogging smoke.

Sophie contemplated the pair in silence for a few moments: obviously locals waiting for the pub to open, she surmised; certainly old enough to remember the war – and hadn't Tom said something about the Americans drinking at this pub? Calling Starsky and Hutch to heel from where they were exploring the hedgerows with great enthusiasm and an orgy of frantic tail-wagging, she walked towards the two men, greeting them with a smiling, 'Good morning.'

One inclined his cloth-capped head in an expressionless nod while the other, who wore an ancient felt hat with a surprisingly jaunty pheasant feather in the greasy band, returned her greeting with a cautious, 'Morning, missus.'

Sophie took a seat on the bench on the other side of the door and leaned towards the pair. 'I've been told there is an old wartime airfield somewhere around here and wondered if you might remember where it is.'

They each began pushing tobacco into their pipes with long bony fingers. 'Ar,' the capped one said eventually, and gave a slow nod. 'There's more 'n one o' them around the Forest.

'Oh ar,' said his companion.

They both fell silent again and shredded a bit more tobacco. Sophie thought she would quite like to bang their heads together. No wonder there was little or no communication between the lively and community-spirited Hawksley and this torpid place, which lacking either church or village hall was really little more than a hamlet. She wondered if the visiting Americans had called it a one-horse town.

She said encouragingly, 'I'm looking for a particular one near here the Americans used during the war.'

Cloth Cap put a match to his pipe and gave a few pulls to get it going before removing it from his mouth to spit on the ground between his feet. Sophie was glad she'd chosen the second bench.

'Ar. Likely that 'ud be the one t'other side of Beechers farm...used to be Ardingly Field when I were a nipper until the Yanks come an' covered it wi' concrete an' give it some fancy name. It's a couple of mile be road...I remember the Yanks used ter come over in them jeeps to the Bull but you can take a short cut across Beechers if yer legs is up to it.' He took another couple of pulls at his pipe then gestured with the stem towards the far corner of the green and a just discernible small pathway leading to a wooden stile. 'If you goes over that stile there, missus an' keep t'path, you'll come out on far side of t'old airfield... it's a fair old stretch, mind you... near on a mile, I reckon.'

'I've plenty of time.' Sophie stood up conscious she must be grinning like an idiot. 'Thank you; thank you very much.' She took some coins from her skirt pocket. 'Please...have one on me,' she said, pressing the money into Cloth Cap's gnarled and bony hand.'

'We will at that, missus,' he said, 'and thank you kindly.'

He watched as Sophie called the dogs to her and set off across the green on eager feet. He nudged his companion. 'Barmy,' he said.

'Oh, ar,' Felt Hat took his pipe from his mouth and spat again. 'She'm barmy alright,' he agreed.

Sophie felt as though she was treading on air as she crossed the green. Of course, it may not actually be the right airfield but the old man hadn't hesitated and there was a good chance she was on the right track. As she swung over the stile she said aloud, 'How about that then, Rupert...I really believe we're going back again; back to your Captain Pop's Falcon Field!'

To her left the path bordered a corn field, all brown furrows now without a spear of green in sight; on her right a skilfully laid hedge ran equally bare of greenery, but there was short, flattened grass beneath her feet and she stepped out strongly, all tiredness temporarily forgotten, while the dogs raced ahead, pausing every few seconds to push their noses into the warren of rabbit burrows beneath the hedge or plunge through it to investigate the sudden pungent and even more exciting smell of fox. Sophie made a mental note to turn the hose on them when they returned to the house, but she didn't really care what they were getting up to; she was so fired with enthusiasm that she couldn't have cared less if they ended up stem to stern in fox excrement.

After all these years, was she really going to stand again where she had stood that day with Rupert; gaze once more down that long runway and know for certain that this was indeed the field from which her father had taken his great aircraft up into the skies on what was destined to be his last ever mission: the one from which he would never return?

Suddenly she found she had reached the end of the path; from here it became no more than a few inches wide of brown earth following the line of what she judged must once have been a perimeter fence. This must be the far side of the airfield, not the wide entrance gate and remains of an old guard post she remembered passing through with Rupert; belatedly she realised she should probably have turned left, not right when she'd emerged from Belstead Wood.

She could see the odd metal pole and traces of steel mesh lying amid the thick grass that crept over the broken concrete, and here and there the faint brick outlines of what must have been barracks, offices and mess halls. Gingerly she stepped over a tangle of steel mesh and began the long walk through wet grass and rubble strewn concrete towards the control tower, standing square and solid at the heart of the airfield, while the two dogs moved back and forth behind her feet as though uncertain about exploring this unfriendly alien landscape.

When Sophie reached the first runway she was surprised to find it in reasonable repair in comparison with the area surrounding it. Although the concrete was crossed at intervals by long grass-filled cracks and any pilot would think twice about using it to take off, it would prove no obstacle to a car or truck. The way her legs and feet were feeling right now, Sophie thought, a car or truck would be welcome, but having come this far she gritted her teeth and soldiered on. Next time, she vowed, she would find a way do the whole journey, both on and off the field, in the Land Rover.

It took her a further ten minutes of rough walking before she finally arrived at the control tower, only to find a chain across the stairway and a notice: UNSAFE STRUCTURE, KEEP OUT. She grimaced. Soon, no doubt, the tower would be demolished as every other building on the site had been and then what might fill these acres – a housing estate; a factory, a new business park? Or would it remain, just another sad abandoned space teeming with the ghosts of those who had lived and worked and flown from here on their deadly missions over Germany?

She sat down on the lower step the dogs moving to position themselves either side of her. Propping an elbow on one knee and cupping her chin in one hand she closed her eyes; thinking back to the summer's day that she and Rupert had climbed these steps together and stood on the platform above; how her brother had leaned his arms on the rusting rail, staring in silence down the runway towards the far end, to the belt of trees and the heath beyond. After a minute or two the memory of that day faded as a different, more intense feeling of melancholy and loss crept over her; almost as though she was sharing another's sorrow, another's pain; as though someone else had sat where she did and poured out their grief and sadness on the unresponsive stone steps.

Ghosts...she thought and shivered and opened her eyes. 'There are no such things as ghosts,' she said aloud and she stood abruptly, startling the dogs, who whined and looked up at her with anxious eyes, so that she stooped to pat their smooth coats and show them that all was well. As she did so her attention was caught by a large hump of grass to one side of the tower. At first glance it looked as if it might be just another heap of rubble covered with grass and weeds but she could see the corner of a stone slab showing through the greenery with what looked like a letter chiselled into the surface. Curiosity aroused she moved closer; yes, it was a definite letter F. She knelt on the damp grass and began to pull at the vegetation, scrabbling with cold fingers until a large rectangular slab of grey stone revealed the words:

FALCON FIELD
USAAC
1942

She sat back on her heels, momentarily unaware that tears were beginning to slide down her cheeks. She had found it at last...the wartime home of Rupert's hero, Captain Pop. The dogs crept nearer, wriggling their warm bodies against her; she put an arm about each and hugged them close and cried for the brother she had lost and the father she had never known.

CHAPTER 14

Later, still sitting on the cold stone step she drank the coffee and ate her lunch, breaking the last scone in half to share between Starsky and Hutch; that done she stood, wrapped her scarf more snugly about her neck and began the long walk home which, as she had eventually managed to locate the main entrance to the airfield, was not such a long walk as before. Cold, with tired, aching feet and weary from her emotional outpouring she longed for two things...a hot bath and the rest of the afternoon in her own company, but as she turned the last bend in the long drive and the manor came in sight she saw a taxi turn from the steps and the unmistakeable figure of Dominic de la Tour vanishing through the open front door.

She stopped dead for a moment as her heart began banging away in her chest, then she began to move again, covering the last fifty yards to the house on feet grown suddenly light. The dogs, catching her change of mood, pranced forward with loud yelps of delight; Dominic heard them and reappeared; he waved then turned, holding out his hand to someone who must have preceded him through the door.

'Sophie, *ma cheer* Sophie...I have a surprise for you and Ben,' he called and he drew to his side the figure of a, slim, blonde woman dressed in the very height of Parisian *haute couturier*. 'I have brought someone special to meet you,' he continued, 'Evette...this is Sophie, my very good friend; Sophie, this is Evette, my wife.'

It was just the moment, Sophie thought ruefully, to be caught out in her boots and old Barbour, her tweed skirt grubby from the dog's paws and smudges of green lichen from the control tower steps. Somehow she carried on up the steps, her eyes after a brief glance at Evette, returned to Dominic. His own eyes were still and watchful and his smile of greeting reached no further than his mouth.

In the short space of time it took her to reach the top of the steps she had steeled herself into an outward calm; although her heart still beat fast she was outwardly the welcoming hostess, putting out her hand to take Evette's rather limp fingers in her own firm, warm hand before accepting Dominic's kiss on both cheeks as though there was nothing unusual in this meeting.

'Ben will be along shortly for his afternoon break so you are just in time to join us...hope you don't mind having tea and cake in the

101

kitchen,' Sophie turned her head to smile at Evette. 'Dominic has probably told you we are a working family and very informal.'

Dominic said: 'Evette doesn't speak much English,' and translated rapidly. Sophie repressed a sigh. *Oh God, not only does the damned woman look like a model from the house of Channel, while I look as though I'm about to go on stage as Eliza Doolittle, but I have to brush up on my French as well...*

To say she was glad to see Ben when he arrived some fifteen minutes later would be an understatement. Since her arrival the exquisite one had had little or nothing to say, possibly due to her somewhat obvious discomfort at sitting at the kitchen table and having her tea served in a mug with the caption PEEL ME A GRAPE, BEAULAH in large purple lettering. Conversation lagged. Dominic was not behaving like Dominic at all while the normally loquacious Mrs Buckley seemed temporarily lost for words. By the time Ben came through the door Sophie had a raging headache and wondered how she was supposed to manage the hours until bedtime. Fortunately the visit would be a short one, as Dominic had already announced they would travel to Cornwall the next morning to spend a few days with his grandparents.

If Ben was at all taken aback to find his best friend and new wife at his kitchen table he didn't show it, but his antenna, always so sensitive where Sophie was concerned, accurately honed in on her discomfort. After greeting their guests he drew out a chair to sit beside her, giving her hand an unobtrusive squeeze. Sophie began to unwind; the first shock was over, Ben was with her; she could do this.

It hadn't exactly been the most relaxed return from her fraught day's outing and when it was time to fetch the twins from the railway station...a task usually performed by Ben... Sophie leaped at his diplomatic suggestion that she should meet them instead, and tensions did ease a little when those two lively characters joined the party. Their delight at Dominic's presence and open curiosity about Evette, on whom they promptly inflicted their schoolboy French, successfully papered over any awkward pauses in the adult conversation.

After the traditional after-school tea and cake had been consumed, Sophie telegraphed Mrs Buckley a brief, telling glance and the housekeeper began to shoo everyone from the kitchen with the excuse that she had the evening meal to prepare. Sophie gave her waist a grateful squeeze as she passed and felt, rather than heard, the housekeepers stifled derogatory snort, her only comment on the very new and devastatingly remote Madame de la Tour.

Ben, Jamie and Xander bore Evette off to the large drawing room and Sophie was both surprised and disconcerted to find Dominic stayed, ostensibly to help herself and Mrs Buckley clear the debris of mugs, plates and cake crumbs from the table and when that was done, followed Sophie out of the kitchen and into the passageway.

'Sophie, I would speak with you alone...please,' he said quietly and after a moment's hesitation she turned from continuing to the drawing room, leading the way instead into the cosy study where a bright fire burned in the grate. He waited for her to be seated in one of the easy chairs beside the hearth before saying abruptly. 'Well, what do you think?'

'What do I think about what?' she said, deliberately obtuse.

He was impatient. 'Evette, of course!'

'Oh,' Sophie hesitated, 'I think she is...exquisite. Congratulations.'

He frowned, said, 'Thank you,' then shrugged and gave a tight smile. 'I am waiting for you to ask: "Why?"'

'Love?' she ventured.

He shrugged again. 'One does not always marry for love, but as Saint Paul said: "It is better to marry than burn."'

'Oh,' Sophie tried for light hearted. 'So did you burn?'

'You know I did – and for whom...'

Suddenly, his eyes, dark and intense were on hers, so filled with meaning that Sophie felt that at any moment she might get a shock from the sheer electric charge of that look. She said breathlessly, 'Some things are better left unsaid...'

'As they have been for...how many years – ten, eleven, twelve? A man can burn for only so long...' He began to prowl about the room. 'You knew, didn't you: that first time we met?'

'Yes, I knew.'

'And you too felt that same thing...that there was a *frisson,* a bond between us?'

'Oh, yes; I felt it alright.'

'And since?'

She didn't answer directly, only said, 'I already had Ben.'

There was a long silence. Pulling at his lower lip Dominic stared into the fire. Eventually he said, 'I am fond of Evette, and she of me; but we are both French – and realists. She is recently divorced and needs a husband who can give her the good things in life to which she is used, which I can and will.' He gave his crooked smile, 'Sophie, soon I shall be forty; it is time to settle down. I need a wife and stability. That is the bargain between us.'

103

Sophie asked gently, 'And that is enough?'

'For now, yes, it is enough.' This time his shrug was eloquent. 'If we are lucky, perhaps we will come to love and it will last; if not, *phfft!*' he waved a hand. '*Que sera, sera*...then I shall burn again!'

She shook her head. 'You must make it last.'

'Yes, I shall work at it...' Suddenly he knelt at her side and placed his hands on her shoulders. '*Ma cheer Sophie...*' his voice was husky, 'I must say this: you are, and will always be, in my heart. I truly wish for you and Ben a long and happy life together; he is still closer to me than any brother; it is a bond we have since childhood that I could never betray, but *how* I wish I had found you first.'

He rose to his feet, drawing her up with him, wrapping her in a close embrace. Sophie could feel his heart pound erratically against her own which was already racing and leaping like a wild thing. For a heady, breathless moment his lips hovered close to hers; then before they could touch she very gently put a hand against his chest, making a space between them.

'This is not very wise,' she said.

He sighed then there was a brief flicker of a smile. 'No,' he said, 'not wise, but a good way to say goodbye.' He kissed her sweetly, gently, on the mouth and stepped back. He said, his voice husky, a little unsteady, 'Now we must join the others. Yes?'

'You go,' conscious that she must have a little time alone she made an easy excuse. 'I need to see Bucky about dinner; I'll be with you all in a few minutes.'

He nodded and left the room; she listened to his retreating footsteps then crossed to the French windows and drawing aside the heavy drapes, opened one of the doors and stepped out onto the terrace.

The light had already gone from the day; it was dark and cold and still, the sky a vast canopy of deep blue velvet pierced with twinkling stars; the paved terrace beneath her feet already sparkling with an early frost. Sophie shivered and tucked her hands into the sleeves of her soft cashmere sweater. Did she feel guilty about that kiss? Of course she did, but was there *really* anything to feel guilty about? The attraction had been there from the beginning, but the love she shared with Ben was far stronger than those occasional, although pleasurable, illicit stirrings Dominic had from time to time aroused in her.

As she watched the sky twin coloured lights came into sight. A plane was flying high; in the silence she imagined she could hear the sound of an engine, which was nonsense of course. Tracing the progress of the lights until the bright pin-points disappeared into the far distance, she wondered if her mother had ever stood where she stood now: watched the giant 'planes from Falcon Field pass overhead on their deadly mission, praying her lover would return safely?

How had they met; when did they become lovers and how long had they been together before Ryan Petersen flew his last and final mission? Had he known then that he was leaving the legacy of a daughter behind?

She murmured aloud: *"Do not despair, for Johnny head-in-air/ he sleeps as sound as Johnny underground/ Fetch out no shroud, for Johnny-in-the-cloud/ and keep your tears for him in after years..."*

"...Better by far, for Johnny-the-bright-star/ to keep your head and see his children fed." Ben finished the verse. 'Starlight and poetry and nostalgia,' he said and Sophie smiled and leaned back against his warm, familiar body, both hands clasping those arms wrapped firmly around her waist.

'I found Falcon Field today,' she said, 'it was a wreck, but I'm glad I found it. The control tower Rupert and I climbed is still standing but it's unsafe and the steps to the roof have been cordoned off.'

'Ah,' he kissed the nape of her neck. 'So that accounts for the Pudney quotation.'

'Have you noticed the poets of the first war wrote mostly about the battlefields and the trenches; those of the second more about war in the air?' she asked. 'Just now when I saw the lights of that 'plane overhead I thought about my mother: how it must have been to see him to fly off, night after night; knowing he might never come back to her. I think I would have died inside every time had that been us.'

'She did it,' he said soberly, 'because there was no alternative: neither of them had a choice. He had to fly and she had to wait and hope. I suppose we all do that in our different ways when we fight our own personal wars.'

There was a wealth of meaning in his voice. For a long moment Sophie was silent, then: 'How long have you known about this...' she hesitated then said bluntly, 'this "thing" between Dominic and me?'

He rubbed his chin on the top of her head. 'Since that first moment you met at the airport. You both looked as though you'd been poll-axed!'

She turned in his arms. 'Did you – do you, mind?'

'Of course,' he looked down at her. 'I wanted to beat the daylights out of him. I was jealous as hell!'

'Was?'

'Yeah – now it's Evette who's jealous as hell; you should have seen the look Dom got when he came into the drawing room – she knew he'd been with you all right.' He leaned his forehead against hers. 'Bet the bugger kissed you tonight!' he said.

'Just a little one – as a sort of farewell; almost brotherly, you might say.'

He tilted her chin. 'How's this for an un-brotherly hello?' he returned.

It was a very long kiss and when it ended, Sophie took his face between her hands and looked deep into those dark brown eyes. 'Now that's what I call a kiss!' she said.

He raised a nonchalant, James Bond eyebrow. 'So it should be. I've been practising on my wife for years!' He took her hands and heeling the terrace door closed drew her back into the room. 'Now eef you weel just step over to thees *couchette*, madame,' he continued in a thick French accent, 'I weel demonstrate further…'

'Oh, *yuk!*' said two voices in unison. Ben and Sophie looked around. Alexander and Jamie stood in the open study doorway wearing identical expressions of extreme disgust. 'If we'd known you were *snogging*,' growled Jamie in his gruff, new man's voice, 'we'd have kept away.'

'Pity you didn't,' commented Ben mildly, 'we were just getting into our stride. What do you want, anyway?'

Xander said, 'We're teaching Evette Australian rummy and we need more players; Uncle Dominic just wants to read and it's no fun with just three.'

Sophie was sceptical. 'Are you sure Evette wants to learn?'

Xanda nodded. 'Yeah…she's OK; she's played *poker*!'

Ben breathed, 'I'll bet she has!' He stood and taking Sophie's hand pulled her to her feet. 'Come on, 'he murmured, 'later on, when our adorable offspring are in bed I might even show the new Madame de la Tour how to play strip Scrabble…that should teach my pal Dominic to keep his kisses for his own wife.'

* * *

Fortunately, no such extreme measure was called for and the remainder of the evening passed in a reasonably relaxed atmosphere. Ben, always an amiable and good humoured host, succeeded in partially thawing Evette's chilly reserve while much to Sophie's

106

amusement, Xanda and Jamie buzzed around Dominic's exotic wife like a pair of testosterone laden honeybees with more pollen than they knew what to do with. As Sophie observed later when she and Ben were getting ready for bed, too much exposure of their sons to such devastating sophistication and the local girls would have a hard time measuring up.

'She is,' as our American cousins would say: "a piece of work".' Ben dropped the second shoe, peeled off his socks and threw them into a corner of the bedroom, 'but very high maintenance, I'd say. Hope Dom can afford her.'

Sophie paused in brushing her hair to look thoughtfully at his reflection in the mirror. 'I noticed he had very little to say about his vineyard this time; usually he tells us all that's been happening there since our last visit. You don't suppose he's thinking of giving it all up and moving somewhere else more in keeping with his new wife's lifestyle: to Paris perhaps?'

'After today, nothing would surprise me.' Ben pulled off his shirt, examined the collar and cuffs, said, 'You'd think I'd been down a coalmine' and threw it after the socks. 'Although I can't see him as part of Parisian cafe society...but then neither can I see Evette working in the vineyard in her spare moments between doing the housewifely bit and raising his children.'

'Or picking up his dirty clothes,' Sophie sighed and went back to brushing her hair, 'you are such a slob, Ben Nicholls.'

He grinned. 'But damnably attractive with it!'

'Yes,' she said, 'there is that.'

'And sweet natured.'

'And sweet natured,' she agreed

'And sexy.'

'That too.'

'So why don't you stop brushing your hair and come to bed?'

Sophie put down the hairbrush, 'Given your sudden interest in getting horizontal this evening,' she said, 'I might start to wonder if exposure to Madame Evette de la Tour has tickled *your* libido more than a little...'

Warm and content, hovering on the edge of sleep, she murmured, 'I had such a strange, unsettling day...finding Falcon Field and all the memories it brought – I sat on the steps on the old control tower and cried buckets, you know; then when I got home, there was Dom arrived out of the blue to stir things up...I felt such a frump beside Evette...but you made it all right for me, how do you always do that?'

107

He said. 'It's a gift...all part of my sweet nature.'

'And your sexiness,' she smiled into the darkness. 'I'm glad they're going tomorrow, are you?'

'Dead right, I am, because if Dom gives you one more of those smouldering looks he's so good at I might have to black both the bugger's eyes.' He put an arm about her waist and pulled her closer. 'I love you and trust you; now go to sleep,' he said.

He lay for a long time listening to her slow, rhythmic breathing; only when he was certain she was fully asleep did he ease his arm from around her shoulders. Sliding out of bed he pulled on his dressing gown and padded silently across the room to sit on the cushioned window seat and look out onto the frosty night. The long case clock in the hallway below struck two deep notes, followed by the tinkling Big Ben chimes. He stared up into the midnight blue sky where a full moon rode high and was glad it was November and the quiet time in the vineyard. All he'd need to do today was a morning and afternoon walk through to check all was well.

It had been a rum old evening, he mused...what a facer to have Dom turning up like that with his Parisian totty; although not such a shock, he guessed, as it had been to Sophie; who could surely have done without *that* particular confrontation at the end of what he knew now had been an emotionally charged day following her discovery of the elusive Falcon Field.

He had liked and respected Geoffrey; had over the years become fond of him, and Pru had been a dear, sweet lady...but for the love of God, whatever had made those two think it was better not to talk about the past; to in effect behave as though the love between Ryan Petersen and Claire de Lacy that had produced the beautiful woman who was now his wife, had never existed...

But it was no use continuing to mull over the past when the present was throwing up some pretty odd problems – Dominic's sudden marriage for starters. What on earth had made him decide to settle down, if that was the word, with a woman like Evette, who must surely be his polar opposite in practically everything – and they'd only met a couple of months ago! Try as he might, Ben could not see her settling to be a country wife in that little cottage by the vineyard. Having travelled a good deal on the continent, particularly in France, he knew a really sophisticated city woman when he saw one, and all he had so far observed, and gleaned in conversation with Dominic's very new wife was that she was a city dweller *par excellence* and definitely high maintenance to boot...so where did that leave Dom, his treasured vineyard and settled way of life?

Rather your problem than mine, pal, he thought, but wished he still had Papa Julius to talk things over with. He missed him so much.

Sophie murmured something in her sleep. Ben left the window, shrugged off his dressing gown and slid back into the bed. She turned and put her arms around him. 'Very nice; very sexy,' she muttered.

'It takes two to tango,' he said and closing his eyes joined her in sleep.

A dozen yards away in their designated bedroom room, Dominic lay wide awake beside his sleeping wife. He would like to have got out of bed, perhaps gone downstairs to read in front of the dying fire, but was loath to disturb and perhaps wake Evette, with the surety that she would resurrect the argument that had raged, albeit in hushed voices, since making their goodnights to Sophie and Ben and coming to bed.

He knew he had been a fool to think he could meet Sophie with Evette at his side and pass it off as a meeting between old friends; knew he hadn't enough guile to carry that through...oh, he'd said the right things, so had Sophie, but *he* had certainly not been able to mask his feelings. Evette, sharp as a stiletto, had immediately picked up on his discomfort and although Sophie had been far better at concealing her own surprise, still it had showed.

He was already regretting his hasty wedding but he'd reached a stage in life when he'd needed more than the casual short term affairs that had satisfied him so far. Ever since that first meeting with Sophie he'd had to acknowledge the fact that he couldn't have her; would never have her, and would probably burn for her the rest of his life. Now after all these years along had come Evette, who was like no other woman he had met and had literally bowled him over. Beautiful, worldly, adept at love, or what passed for it between the sheets, and, in her way, undemanding; apart that was from the expectation to be wined and dined and seen in the right places, which had at first both amused and intrigued him. But the first flush of passion was already over and problems beginning to loom. He was neglecting his vineyard, soon, if matters didn't improve, he would have to employ a manager to oversee the day to day running of it. Evette had made it clear country living was not for her by spending the previous week looking at apartments in Paris.

Dominic moved restlessly; thought what a fool he'd been and tried to banish the recurring agonizing image of Sophie sleeping in Ben's arms.

CHAPTER 15

Hampshire, December 1979

It was the first Christmas Charles and Caroline de la Tour had come alone to Hawksley.

'Hélène sends her love, but she is spending the holiday in Orleans with the family of her new fiancé,' Caro informed Sophie, kissing her on both cheeks.

'...And our idiot son is skiing in Austria with Evette and her cronies,' Charles added with heavy sarcasm then turned to Ben. 'So, I can once again flirt with your beautiful wife without hindrance, yes?' and gave his disarming grin

'As much as *your* beautiful wife allows,' Ben agreed.

Caro slipped her arm through Sophie's. 'I think we shall enjoy being a smaller party: we can eat, talk, walk with the dogs – and without Dominic egging your sons on to endless cut-throat card games, ration the number we're willing play, and in the evenings after they've gone to bed we can drink too much wine and fall asleep in front of the television...' she gave her throaty chuckle, 'or do those big handsome boys stay up now and drink with us?'

'Not likely,' said Ben firmly, 'at fifteen the only thing that sparkles in their glasses is coca cola and they've the sense to take themselves off to bed when the conversation gets too boringly adult.'

After all the festivities and food and present giving of Christmas Day Alexander wandered into his brother's room that evening, observing with provocative innocence, 'It's been a funny sort of Christmas without Uncle Dominic; he's always been so keen to come. Simply can't think why he went skiing this year, can you?'

Jamie said 'You jest, of course; the luscious Evette wouldn't let him.'

Alexander grinned. 'Pity; I wouldn't have minded seeing her again.'

'Nor me, she's hot stuff, I bet.' Jamie clasped his hands behind his head and leaned back against the pillows, 'but it wouldn't have been much fun if she'd come. You can tell she gives Uncle Charles and Aunt Caro the pip; dad doesn't like her much either and neither does mum – and Evette hates *her.*'

'Yeah,' Alexander perched on the end of his brother's bed,

110

tucking his feet beneath his dressing gown. 'She hates mum all right.' He grinned. 'I wonder why?'

'It might possibly be that Uncle Dominic fancies her!'

'You don't say…amuses dad no end when the flirty looks start,' he gave a reminiscent sigh. 'I quite miss watching old Dom at it, with ma enjoying it and dad watching from the side-lines.'

'Pity he can't come without bloody Evette,' Alexander gave a disgusted snort, 'but if he did I imagine she'd make his life hell.'

'Blimey – women, I'll make damned sure I don't land one of the bossy ones.' Jamie slid down under the bedclothes until only his eyes and nose showed. 'Bugger off will you, Xanda. I need my kip…got the Boxing Day rugger match tomorrow afternoon – it's traditional.'

'You really are a moron,' Alexander said loftily, 'but it's OK, I'm going. God knows, you need all the beauty sleep you can get when you keep having your face stepped on and your ears squashed every weekend; you should be like me and stick to rowing. It's a lot safer.'

'But rugby pulls more girls,' Jamie jeered, 'only the dog-faces hang around the boat sheds.'

'At least they are dog-faces with class, rather than touch-line tarts.' Alexander gathered his dressing gown around him and retreated to the peace of his own room, where he jumped into bed, his cold feet scrabbling for the hot water bottle.

He thought about Evette. She was hot all right; she had what Papa Julius would have called 'It', his feet curled like simian paws around the cooling hot water bottle. He missed Papa Julius and wondered what he would have thought of Evette. Not much, probably. Alexander sighed. She was a sexy woman all right; she looked good and smelled even better but was way out of league for a not-yet-sixteen year old guy.

But he could quite see why old Dom had fallen for her.

PART THREE

1980–1986

THE END OF THE BEGINING

'You've got to give a little, take a little,
Let your poor heart break a little.
That's the story of, that's the glory of Love.'

Billy Hill

CHAPTER 16

Hampshire, July 1982

In the late afternoon of a day of blue skies and scorching sun Dominic came again to Hawksley. He came alone in the breathless hush between day and evening, when shadows ran long across the lawns and the sweet smell of the summer's day lingered in the air.

Along with a half dozen of their longest established resident friends, Sophie and Ben were relaxing in lazy content on garden chairs set around the wrought iron table beneath the trees, tall glasses of iced coffee before them, chatting of holidays already taken and those still to come. Starsky and Hutch and a brace of other canines friends sprawled dozing beneath the table until the crunch of gravel roused them to sudden noisy life and they leaped up to rush around the side of the house barking hysterically.

'What the....' Ben rose to his feet as the intruder appeared, surrounded by barking, leaping dogs. He clapped a theatrical hand to his heart, as though about to faint. 'Will you just look at what's climbed from under a rock?'

'What a friend... and call off these noisy hounds.' Dominic strolled across the lawn, kissed Sophie on both cheeks and clasped Ben's hand. Ben introduced him to their neighbours and he bowed, said 'Enchanté,' to the women, shook hands with the men and took a seat as though it was the most natural thing in the world for him to just amble up and join the party.

Sophie was speechless, so amazed by his sudden appearance after so long that for a few moments she was unaware that for the first time she hadn't experienced that insidious little kick inside that the sight of him had always prompted.

But he was changed; no longer the Dominic of three years ago who had appeared with Evette at his side. Now his face had lost its habitual weather beaten tan and was paler and more noticeably lined, with a scattering of grey hair already showing at his temples. His eyes no longer snapped with laughter but were very still, their expression unfathomable, giving no hint of his inner thoughts and feelings.

She realised she had been holding her breath and let it go slowly, and she hoped, silently. She held up the jug of coffee. 'You look as though you could use a glass of this,' she said.

He smiled. 'Yes, I am thirsty...I came only to the village by taxi. I thought I would walk and see how things may have changed. It has been a long time.'

'Three years too long,' Ben rested a hand on his shoulder, 'we have missed you,' he said simply.

'And I you, my good friends,' he looked around. 'Where is your wonderful Madame Buckley – where also are the young men?'

'Bucky is staying a few days with her sister in Essex looking at houses.' Sophie's smile was rueful. 'Darling Bucky; she's almost reached her three score years and ten and still *very* reluctant to retire and we've really had to insist she does sooner rather than later. We'd love to have her stay right where she is in her own apartment and put her feet up, but she'll never do that at Hawksley. Her sister wants them to join forces and find a place together by the sea and that seems to ring all the right bells with her...the two of them have always been close; good friends as well as sisters, so we're all keeping our fingers crossed...as for the boys,' Sophie laughed, '*They* are spending the summer abroad. Jamie's in New Zealand working as a 'gofer' at a Private Flying Club for free flying instruction when and where he can get it, and of course, playing Rugby whenever he gets the chance. Xander's in California working his way through the best vineyards in the state and also, we suspect through the choicest girls California has to offer. We try not to think how either of them might be spending their spare time.'

By now evening was settling firmly into place and one by one the guests made their farewells and returned to their own apartments, leaving Sophie, Ben and Dominic alone in the gathering dusk

Dominic looked at them over the rim of his glass. 'You can ask,' he said, 'it doesn't hurt anymore.' He gave a little grimace, 'well, not much.'

'Who left whom – and when?' Ben asked.

'Evette went – four months ago. I have not yet told Caro or papa. In a little while I will. Somehow I wanted to tell you first...' he hesitated and spread his hands, 'to bridge the gap. It has been a long time.'

'We know from Caro and Charles things have not gone well between you and Evette. They've been worried sick,' Ben frowned. 'That manager you put in at the vineyard hasn't been up to the job either. You've lost a lot of business.'

Dominic shrugged. 'To grow good grapes is a gift; to sell the product is hard work; he had neither the gift nor the inclination to hard work. It will take time to recoup my losses; a good reputation once lost is hard to regain.'

116

'What caused the break-up between you and Evette?' Sophie was in no mood for diplomacy, rather she was irritated by his air of *laissez faire*. As if a failed marriage and a declining business were matters of no importance. *I'd quite like to kick him,* she thought. Aloud, she said: 'Did she find someone else or did you just get fed up with Paris?'

'Oh,' he shrugged again, that expressive Gallic shrug which at that moment she found particularly irritating. 'Yes, she found someone richer and more interesting, and yes, I found Paris tedious. Fine to visit; hell to live in.' He wrinkled his nose. 'Noisy; it stinks and the pavements are covered in dog shit.'

Ben laughed, which irritated Sophie even more. Just like the chaps to hang together and make light of it all. She said with silky sarcasm, 'So how long did you "work at it?" How long before you said, "*Que sera, sera*" and Evette decided to walk away?'

Ben looked puzzled. 'What's that supposed to mean. Soph?'

She stood, picked up the tray with the empty jug and glasses. 'Ask Dominic – he knows what it means,' she said and turned and walked towards the house.

They watched her walk away; Ben raised enquiring brows and for once Dominic forbore to shrug, instead he spread both hands again, this time in defeat. 'I think, as you would say, I had that coming to me!' He shook his head. 'That first time I came with Evette, we talked, Sophie and I. You must have known from the beginning how I felt about Sophie, yes? For the first time that night I told her I loved her but knew she loved only you. I said Evette and I were not in love but that I was fond of her as she was of me; that we were both realists and we had an arrangement: she would give me stability and a family life, I in turn would provide the lifestyle to which she was accustomed.'

Ben said, 'That sounds like a dichotomy of interests bound to end in disaster!'

Dominic gave a wry smile. 'As so it proved. I said then that if we were lucky it would last; Sophie told me I must make it last and I said I would. As you see, I failed. Evette found the family life too hard a price to pay and I could not become accustomed to her lifestyle. So – now it is over, and your Sophie she is out of patience with me.'

'And rightly so, you idiot, but don't worry – she'll forgive you, eventually!' Ben stood, giving his friend's shoulder and affectionate squeeze. 'Come on, we'll be eating soon but Sophie's arranged a cold meal tonight so we've time to treat ourselves to something a little more interesting than iced coffee before we eat.'

It really was like old times, Sophie thought as they sat around the dinner table that evening, almost as though Dominic had never been absent, had never dropped his bombshell on that cold November day before slipping away, out of sight and sound; leaving a gaping empty space in all their lives. Now that space was filled again and she felt a great upsurge of pleasure, very different, she realised, from those former illicit little stirrings of guilty passion his presence had always provoked. Now she was comfortable that she still cared for him, although in a different way, could accept him for what he was and enjoy his company while she worked on this new relationship.

She hoped he felt the same way, but with Dominic, one could never be sure.

* * *

He left after a week, aware that his relationship with Sophie had changed; that she had effected the change without needing to put it into words and he stayed carefully within the boundaries of this new friendship, while acknowledging with wry despair that his feelings for her hadn't changed. *'Que sera, sera,'* he muttered as he boarded his plane, 'but my feelings must take the back seat from now on and at least I have learned I must keep them to myself!'

He sat in his designated place in the aircraft and thought about his last sight of her: how she'd stood at the end of the platform as the train started to move; how he'd hung out of the train window, waving; how Ben's arm lay about her shoulders as they each raised an arm in farewell; how her hair shone in the bright sunlight, her slender form in checked shirt and jeans outlined against the clear blue sky...

The plane began to move and he closed his eyes. It was over; he was going home; back to tend his vines and salvage his neglected business, to make his peace with his parents; to start life all over again. He hoped the new man in Evette's life would make her happier than he had managed; she was an OK woman; honest about what she felt and wanted. And they had had fun, quite a lot of it along the way, and they'd tried; tried really hard and long but in the end the sensible arrangement had failed and they had simply drifted apart. Without love it just hadn't been enough for either of them.

Opening his eyes he looked out of his window as the plane finished climbing and began to level out; the familiar contours of the land giving way to the sea until that too was lost to sight beneath white sunlit clouds. He sighed. *Au revoir, Sophie je t'aime...*he glanced up as the flight attendant passed down the aisle. His eyes travelled from her jaunty cap to her trim ankles before returning to linger on her legs. Not bad, he thought with a stirring of interest; not bad at all, in fact very good...but perhaps not quite good enough.

He settled back into his seat, wondering if and when he would ever get Sophie Nicholls out of his head and heart.

CHAPTER 17

London, November 1983

Sophie paused at the arch to the Burlington Arcade, looked at her watch and gave an exasperated sigh. She'd done all the shopping she wanted but it had taken longer than expected, if only she hadn't got the oldest and slowest shop assistant in Dickens and Jones she'd have been at Waterloo in time for the early train. Now the rush hour was in full swing and by the time she'd found a taxi, which would be bound to take her on the longest, most congested route to the station, she'd find herself on a crowded commuter train with the likelihood of standing most, if not all of the way. The days when a gentleman would give up his seat to a lady were long gone; nowadays it was every man, and woman, for his or her self.

And quite right too, she thought virtuously, we females were the ones who fought for equality; no use moaning about it now it's here. She would while away an hour or so until the rush was over with a late tea at the Strand Corner House, which was close by and somewhere a lone female, even a lone forty plus female, wouldn't be mistaken for either an easy pick-up or a lush looking for the offer of a free martini, such as had happened once in the Savoy, where much to Ben's delight while he was in the gents she had been propositioned by a portly Brigadier.

When she reached the Corner House it was busy; many of the patrons like her were female and burdened with several shopping bags, grateful for the opportunity to rest their aching arms and feet. When the Joe Lyons equivalent of the Savoy concierge materialised from behind a desk to ask if she would mind sharing a table, Sophie sighed inwardly but smiled, said that would be fine and was shown to a table for two already occupied by a young woman wearing faded jeans and a white Shetland jersey under a brown corduroy jacket. As Sophie approached, the young woman swept a well-travelled canvas grip from the second chair and gave a broad grin.

'Hi,' she said, 'you sure are welcome – thought I might get stuck with some boring old guy offering to show me the sights of London!'

Sophie grinned in return, 'It can happen,' she seated herself and after stowing her various bags and boxes on the floor beside her took a closer look at her companion.

Mid to late twenties, she guessed, by the accent obviously American, although there was a hint of something crisper in her speech than that of the average US citizen; she had an attractive lively face topped with short, slightly curling mid-brown hair, while a pair of remarkably keen, intelligent brown eyes completed the picture. A pleasing, and interesting face, Sophie thought, then realised the girl was making much the same inventory of her. She laughed aloud as their eyes met and held out her hand.

'Sophie Nicholls...up from Hampshire and combining my bi-annual shop with some odds and ends for Christmas,' she said.

'Nicole Frasier, from New England: over from the States for a week or so on a much needed break from the rat race.' She had a firm, confident handshake.

'What particular part of the rat race?'

'The newspaper and magazine industry...I'm a free-lance journalist.'

Sophie was intrigued. She gave her a long look. 'Not fashion or beauty, I bet.'

'Dead right; I'm mostly employed as a war correspondent... anyone starts trouble any place and I'm there. I was in on your Falklands thing...pretty rough and hellish noisy!'

Sophie grimaced. 'London isn't always the place to be looking for a peaceful break,' she observed. 'I don't think the IRA will have quite finished with us yet – you could be as likely to be blown up here as you were in Port Stanley.'

'Yeah...our TV was full of all the bombing a couple of years back...all those men – and the poor horses...gee, you should have seen my mom, she was in tears, so was I – I come from London, you know; lived here 'till I was ten, when my ma fell in love with a Yankee Professor from New England and we moved to the States.'

'I thought I detected a touch of the Brit when you first spoke,' Sophie smiled. 'Do you have relatives over here?'

'Not now, we all used to come every summer vacation to visit the grandparents down in Devon, but my grandma, who believe it or not was my step-dad's *mother,* died back in seventy-nine and my grandpa a few months later. My step-brother Joel and I spent a couple of weeks with ma sorting their place in Devon – shipping some things home, you know and getting the rest sold; that was the last time we came back.' She paused while the waitress came to take their orders before continuing: 'I went down last week to take a look around the old place but was all a bit sad and I only stayed a day; I'm not one for wallowing in nostalgia. Besides, I love London,' she grinned. 'Like

Sinatra says of Chicago – it's my kind of town!'

'How much longer are you staying here?'

'This is my last day...things look like they might be hotting up in Chile sometime soon; I've booked a flight home tomorrow so I can be ready if anything blows.'

Sophie felt a slight stab of disappointment. She liked Nicole Frasier; there was something very engaging about her; she'd even been on the verge of asking her down to Hawksley for a few days, but she recognised a true restless spirit when she saw one; Jamie was the same; always seeking, always reaching for the next adventure...she gave an involuntary smile at the thought of her son.

'Say,' her companion was staring at her, her forehead wrinkled in puzzlement, 'don't I know you from someplace...I been wondering ...you look kind of familiar.'

'I shouldn't think so,' Sophie smiled again and shook her head. 'I don't know any Americans.'

'There, you've done it again!' Nicole Frasier knocked her forehead with a clenched fist. 'It's the smile...well, not only that. Gee, I wish I could remember....' She looked at Sophie earnestly, 'hey, you're not famous, are you – like an actress – or a writer: something like that?'

'Lord, no,' Sophie laughed out loud, 'no such luck!'

Nicola let out an exasperated breath. 'You ever been Boston way? – or New York?' and when Sophie shook her head again she sat back in her chair, looking at her with narrowed eyes. 'This is going to bug me like hell,' she said, 'but it'll come to me because you surely do remind me of someone.'

Sophie couldn't help but be amused. 'When you do remember I rather hope it *is* someone famous; I've never been confused with anyone special before.'

Nicole gave her wide, engaging grin. 'If I do and it is someone special I'll mail you: Mrs Sophie Nicholls, care of...where is it you live?'

'Hawksley, Hampshire...that should get me,' Sophie answered with mock solemnity. 'Simply *everyone* there knows who I am!'

They spent a pleasant, unhurried hour or so over their meal, Nicole was intrigued by Sophie Nicholls and her life in Hampshire; being a very good journalist she could picture the old house, the vineyard, the twin boys and a husband called Ben and felt a pang of genuine disappointment when Sophie glanced at her watch and said, 'Heavens, I'd better start looking for a taxi; if I miss too many trains my husband will be calling out a search party.' Signalling to a passing waitress she smiled, miming writing a bill for both meals then began gathering her bags together. 'This is on me,' she said, as the waitress handed her the bill, 'for being such a good companion...' and held up a hand as Nicole began to protest, 'I insist; after all, you might have saved *me* from being landed with some boring old guy.' She stood, smiling and offering her hand. 'Goodbye, Nicole, I've enjoyed your company very much. Have a safe journey home tomorrow.'

'Cheers, Sophie.' Again the handshake was firm and confident, 'and thanks – if I come over again I'll look you up in Hawksley, Hampshire, and the meal will be on me!'

She watched Sophie Nicholls thread her way through the tables towards the entrance, pause to pay at the counter, then turn and wave before disappearing through the doors and out into the night. Beautiful smooth walk, she thought; beautiful graceful woman. Late thirties, she hazarded; maybe just a touch older; with those looks and that figure it was difficult to tell. With an unexpected twinge of envy she thought it must be nice to look like that and be going home to those twin boys and a husband who would be worried if she was late...

Nicole sighed, retrieved her canvas grip from the floor and went out into the combined smells of exhaust fumes, sooty buildings and the all-pervasive miasma of lingering damp that was London on a winter's evening.

If only she hadn't booked tomorrow's flight, she would quite like to have seen more of her erstwhile table companion. ..

"Hawksley, some place in Hampshire..." those words, uttered in that so very English voice stirred something deep down in her brain; for a moment she stood lost in thought, catching at the coat tails of memory. Surely she'd heard the name Hawksley before somewhere, but to her knowledge she had never set foot in Hampshire, and not met Sophie Nichols until an hour or so ago, so why had both Sophie's looks and the place she lived triggered that sudden instinctive response... Nicole shook her head. No point in burdening her brain with it all right now: as dad would say: *"Not to worry, cupcake, it'll come to you soon...it'll come."* Nicole smiled as she thought of dad and his easy words of comfort. It was the sort of thing he'd say when she was a little girl, struggling to lean the pledge to the flag they recited in her new school each morning, or when she was baffled by the strange spelling of everyday words, the philosophical advice always delivered in that soft, laid back New England drawl.

Hadn't he been stationed somewhere in the south of England during the war? She searched her memory for anything relevant she might have heard. Perhaps he'd come across this place Hawksley sometime and just mentioned it in passing: that was probably it, she thought, she'd always had a very retentive memory.

But that still didn't explain why she was so sure she'd seen Sophie Nicholls before...

Sophie had 'phoned Ben before she boarded the later train and he was waiting on the platform when the train pulled in. He kissed her and hugged her hard. 'By the time you rang me I was beginning to think you'd run off with a strapping young guardsman,' he said.

She kissed him back. 'These days I wouldn't consider anything less than a millionaire film star – or at a pinch a really good-looking and equally wealthy Rugby player.'

He put an arm about her shoulders. 'You'd be lucky to find one of those without a broken nose and cauliflower ears,' he said. 'Come along, you can tell me in the car all about the exciting time you had buying my shirts and underpants.'

She said, 'I didn't spend an entire day shopping for you.'

'I bet you didn't...for a start my shirts and pants are unlikely to be nestling in this whopping great carrier from Dickens and Jones, nor the pink one with solid gold logo from Flossie's fashions, or any other of these colourful and expensive looking plastic holdalls – my God,' he held up a large, silver and white stripped box, 'this one's the size of a cabin trunk; how did you manage all these at Waterloo?'

'I found a porter – and I had such a lovely time in Simpsons where a young man tried to sell me a pink shirt with a very long pointy collar and embroidery down the front...you would have loved it...' she slapped his hand as he began peering and rummaging in one of the larger plastic carriers. 'Don't look; there are Christmas prezzies in there!'

* * *

Once back at Hawksley, seated in the drawing room on the marvellously squashy old sofa before a blazing fire, with a plate of ham sandwiches on the coffee table beside her and a glass of wine in her hand, Sophie kicked off her shoes and putting her feet up gave a great sigh of contentment. 'Such luxury; you are a husband in a million,' she said.

'I know,' Ben raised his glass, 'that's why I now have four posh shirts from Gieves and Hawkes, some very snazzy underpants and a half dozen pairs of Argyll socks that would look great on a golf course but just a touch out of place in a vineyard...Now what is it you're bursting to tell me? I could hear your brain buzzing all the way home.' He sat down and began massaging her feet.

Sophie wriggled her toes and settled back into the cushions. 'I shared a table in Joe Lyons with a most unusual American,' she began.

'Handsome and rich, was he?' Ben interrupted, 'bet he was called Elmer or Hank or Orvis.'

'Wrong sex – and don't be so parochial,' Sophie chided, '*she* was a very attractive young woman – a journalist, and what the boys would call a dish.'

'And – '

'She said I had a familiar face and thought I might be someone famous, like an actress. I felt quite flattered.' Sophie fluttered her eyelashes and Ben laughed. 'Her name is Nicole Frasier,' she continued, 'and she hails from New England; quite a tough girl in her way; she's a war correspondent.'

'Wow!' said Ben.

Sophie grinned 'She covered the Falklands; said it was hellish noisy!'

'Tell me more,' said Ben.

So she did, recounting as faithfully as she could the gist of their conversation. 'I had to leave her to catch my train,' she finished, 'and I know this probably sounds odd, but there was just *something* about her – I can't pin down what it was...' she wrinkled her brow, 'after all, we were just a couple of strangers sharing a table for an hour or so, but she looked so tough, but at the same time so vulnerable, that if she hadn't a flight booked for tomorrow morning I would have invited her back here tonight.' She gave an embarrassed laugh, 'Silly, isn't it?'

'No, just very you,' Ben gave her a quizzical look, 'but it sounds as though she might have jumped at the chance if you had,' he said.

Sophie said thoughtfully, 'I don't know, she didn't say much about herself at all; only that she'd been born in London and her father died when she was very young; then her mother married an American Professor of European Literature from Boston or thereabouts and moved to the States. In fact, now I come to think back, she spent most of the time asking about me and life at Hawksley.'

'Sweetheart, that's what journalists do.' Ben finished massaging her feet and reached for his wineglass. 'One day when she's hard up she'll turn it into an: "aren't these Brits just so cute and old-fashioned" sort of article for some glossy magazine.'

'Somehow I don't think so; it was nice though to chat again with someone so interesting – and *young.* ' Sophie stretched and sighed. 'I do miss the boys. Jamie seems to love every minute of his time at Oxford but I worry a little about Xander; he seems a rather lost at Cirencester.'

Ben grunted. 'Well, he chose agricultural College over University ...and it's only the Farm Management Course he's less than enthusiastic about, but if he aims to run this place himself when I'm in my dotage he'll need to get to grips with the business side of agriculture. Whether it's growing corn or grapes...the day to day problems of making things pay in a business that relies on the English weather for success or failure are all pretty much the same.'

'Oh, he'll manage,' said Sophie comfortably, 'you did.'

CHAPTER 18

Boston, Connecticut, New England, November 1983

Joel was waiting at Logan airport; leaning against a kiosk in the foyer reading a Robert B. Parker paperback, his thick, mahogany colour hair standing out like a beacon, his tall broad-shouldered figure dressed as usual in leather jacket, sweatshirt, washed out jeans and loafers without any socks.

'Hi, bro,' Nicole leaned and kissed his cheek, which was cold and smelt of the ocean, 'how's my favourite beach bum.'

'Been taking a rest for a couple weeks before sailing a millionaire's spanking new yacht to the Bahamas 'cause his little princess fancies having a Christmas beach wedding there.'

'She could have had that with a lot less expense and hassle in California,' she commented, 'and why sail when flying is faster?'

He grinned and took her holdall. 'Kid, you just don't understand millionaires...the yacht trip's so as him and his pals can have a real good time getting stoned all the way there and back.'

She gave a disparaging sniff. 'As dad would say: "Prostituting yourself as usual to the filthy rich!"'

'Yeah,' he grinned again, 'but it's more fun and pays better than the Navy.'

'How *are* mum and dad?' she asked as they left the concourse and made their way over to the parking lot.

'OK, they enjoyed one of their flack-attacks last night, with your mom getting mad as hell saying it was time you settled down and quit roaming around the world trying to get your head shot off, and dad stirring the pot by saying as you and she were like as two peas in a pod and stubborn as a pair of mules she might as well save her breath.' Joel grinned reminiscently, 'I sure do enjoy hearing them still at it; reminds me of when we were kids and makes me forget they're gettin' older.'

By now they had reached his less than pristine green 1980 Lincoln convertible and he paused for a moment, resting her bag on the hood. 'You know, sis, mom could be right...we all do worry like hell about you; most of the people in the places you go don't give a rat's arse whether you tell the world about them or not – and they'll still be fighting each other when you're old and sittin' on the porch in your rocking chair.' He hunched his shoulders at the sudden steely

127

look in her eyes. 'Hell, Nic, why go on risking your life in some God-forsaken place where they'd cut your throat soon as look at you if they thought you weren't on their side?'

She said stubbornly 'I tell it as it is; I think I make a difference.'

'That may be how you see it, but from where I stand, apart from the odd assignment to a real war zone like the Falklands, the sort of things you risk your life for are little more than old Tribal disputes that have been going on since Creation, only now they have mortar bombs and Kalashnikovs in place of flint spears and sling shots.'

She didn't answer him but sat in moody silence as he negotiated his way through the parking lot and out into the snarl of traffic around the airport, but when they had eventually cleared the city and were on the two lane highway she half turned toward him and asked, 'Joel, do you remember where it was dad did his service in the UK?'

'Not really; he never talks about it, does he?' he wrinkled his brow in thought. 'I got a feeling it was somewhere in the south.'

'Might it have been Hampshire?'

'No idea – although, hang on a minute...' he broke off to cross lanes to get ahead of a truck then continued, 'Remember that Christmas we were all at your grandpa's in Devon and dad and your mom told us they were getting married and coming back here to live?'

'Oh, yeah,' Nicole started to laugh, 'we weren't best pleased, were we?'

'Nah...I near wet my pants because I knew I'd never survive if the guy's back home found out you were aiming to marry me.'

'We were only ten!' she protested. 'I didn't know any better.'

'Well, any road...after you and me had a punch-up and things kind of settled down again, him and your mom took off for a weekend together, remember?'

'Yes,' she giggled, 'and after they'd left we came back in from sledding and found my grandpa and your grandma nestled up close on the couch.'

'Proves you can never be too old to neck,' he said dryly. 'Well sometime while they were away over that weekend I remember I was snooping around the kitchen looking for cookies and heard gran'ma say something about she hoped dad going back to Hampshire again wouldn't stir a hornet's nest of trouble.'

'So...' Nicole was thoughtful, '...if you and your dad were living in London back then – when was it – sixty-five, sixty-six? – and it was your first visit; the only time *he'd* have been in Hampshire before then must have been during the war...Oh boy,' she enthused, 'this is beginning to sound like a detective story!'

'Maybe I could help if you told me the plot,' Joel suggested as they reached the New Hampshire borders, taking the highway towards the coast and Bracket Sound.

'There isn't one, really,' she confessed, 'but just before I came back I got chatting to a woman who came from a place in Hampshire called Hawksley. She looked so familiar I thought at first she was maybe someone famous, but it wasn't *that* sort of familiarity; more like someone I knew really well but I just couldn't get it at the time and it really bugged me. I thought about her all the way back on the plane then suddenly it came to me... ' she stopped and gave an embarrassed little laugh. 'I know you're going to tell me I'm a real idiot, but Joel, she looked just like dad!'

He grinned, 'She was *that* old?'

'God, no; only around her late thirties, I'd guess, really *really* silvery blonde hair and those sort of sculpted, Nordic looks, exactly like his...and her *eyes*...well, they were the dead image of dad's...when I think how he looked twenty years or so back, they could have been brother and sister or even – JOEL!'

She snatched at his arm so suddenly that the car swerved. He swore loudly. 'What the fuck...'

'Pull over,' she said tersely, 'pull over *now*.'

'Hell, why,' he protested, 'in a little over twenty and we're right home.'

'I can't say this at home...look,' she gestured as a gas station with an adjoining diner came into sight, 'stop there; we can have a coffee and talk. I've got to get this out right now or my head'll explode.'

'And muck my car seats – that's gross,' he mocked, but slowed and turning from the road slid the Lincoln to rest between a truck and a sleek Mercedes before leading the way into the diner. When they were seated and their coffee on the table, he leaned back and folded his arms. 'OK,' he said, 'now shoot.'

Nicole took a deep breath. 'I'm not just saying this off the top of my head,' she said slowly and deliberately, 'but she *could* have been his daughter – Joel, do you realise that back in the good old UK, *you* could have a half-sister your dad never owned to.'

'Yeah, and pigs might fly,' he scoffed. 'You've sure got some imagination, kid.'

'I'm serious. You haven't seen her...and isn't the timing bang on? If I'm right about her age, given a year or so either way she'd have been born , or at least conceived, around the time dad was in the UK.'

'Not a chance,' Joel was emphatic, 'He's too straight, always has

129

been. He'd never have had someone he cared enough about to have an affair with then left her alone to carry the load.'

'But, Joel, one thing we do know is that he was shot down over France and went missing for near on a year – remember Grandma Hanna telling us everyone thought he was dead? Maybe, just maybe, he never knew about the baby, and if the woman, whoever she is that dad was having the affair with was told, same as your grandma, that he was dead, she wouldn't have gone looking for him, would she?'

'That's one hell of a big maybe. Even if you're right...and I don't think you are, if he doesn't know he has a daughter, how you figuring on finding out for sure? Nobody ever got much information out of my dad about what he did in the war, or where he did it – and I can't see even you changing that.'

Nicola chewed her lip, two vertical frown lines appearing between her brows. 'I'll find out,' she said tersely, 'don't you worry; I'll find out if means I have to go back to England and track down Mrs Sophie Nicholls, who lives in someplace called Hawksley in Hampshire.'

Joel looked at her over his coffee cup. 'Dream on, kid...that could be one of those big old UK towns you could search until you were bat-eyed and still not find her.' He put down his cup to lean across the table, his green eyes suddenly earnest. 'Look, Nic, even suppose you're right and this Sophie -what's-her-name *is* his daughter, what good will it do either of them to find it out all these years later? Her mother probably married someone else and this Sophie may not even know *who* her father was, except he's dead. That's the way things were during the war; not all the girls the guys slept with became GI Brides!'

She said stubbornly, 'You ever thought dad might already have found out about her sometime and went looking? The place can't be all that big: the woman said if I ever came to the UK again I should look her up; that everyone in Hawksley knew who she was.'

'OK, OK...so maybe he did find out somehow; but just tell me this: if dad went down to this place in Hampshire when we were over there in the 'sixties to look up his old girlfriend and check if he left a little something behind last time around, why would he take your mom with him? – So as he could roll up and say, '"Hi, honey, I know you were probably told I was dead, and I'm sorry about the kid, but hey, here I am – oh, and by the way, meet the future Mrs Peterson?"'

She said glumly, 'Well, put like that, it does sound kind of crazy.'

'That's because it is.' He took her hand and gave it a little squeeze. 'Take my advice for once, will you, Nic? Forget about

Hampshire, England and stick with New England, USA. Go off on your next little jaunt to some other trouble spot and by the time you've filed your first copy you'll have forgotten all about that blonde, blue-eyed Brit you found in London.'

She sighed. 'Uh-huh – guess you're right,' she agreed with suspicious docility, although her eyes had that old familiar far-away look that Joel both knew and mistrusted. But for now at least, he figured, the likelihood of her stirring a whole shit load of trouble soon as they hit home had been avoided...but he wouldn't bet more than a nickel that her sharp, inquisitive brain wouldn't keep worrying away at the subject of his dad's possible wartime romance...and the daughter he might or might not have had.

He took a long thoughtful sip at his coffee. He certainly wasn't going to admit to Nicole that the name Hawksley did have a kinda familiar ring, and that if he thought real hard he might just be able to remember where he'd heard it before...

But with luck he'd be up and way across the ocean before he remembered; well away from any chance he might open his big mouth and have the shit fly in his direction.

CHAPTER 19

Bracket Sound, Connecticut, November 1983

Ryan stood at the porch window looking out to where the ocean swelled gently under the light of a full moon, the only sound the faint susurration of waves as they broke along the shore. Behind him in the kitchen the radio played softly: Ella Fitzgerald singing, 'God Bless the Child.' The night was so still he could hear a car shift gears out front preparatory to climbing the steep hill behind the main street. A calm night; one to cherish and remember when the winter storms reached full strength and the ocean rolled across the harbour to fling it's might against the stout piles that held the rear of the house high above the beach. But right now New England was perfect; a glory of red and gold and green still tuning the wooded hills above the Sound into some kind of fantastic futuristic painting; as though an artist had loaded his brushes with colour and dabbed them randomly over a huge canvas.

Summer or winter, he loved his house; wouldn't want to live anywhere else; here he had soldiered on through bad times as well as good; had watched helplessly as his young wife slid deeper and deeper into the depression that had, after too many years to bear thinking about, finally ended in her death. Here he had battled his guilt because he hadn't loved her enough, and in compensation tried too hard to love their son and for a while failed miserably at that too...

But in the end, he had loved Joel; with pride watched him grow to manhood; seen him join the Navy rather than wait to be drafted, because he loved the sea and everything to do with it; then later decided the discipline of a sailor's life was not for him and left the service for the easier option of navigating luxury yachts around the world for owners who had not the wit or skill to sail themselves.

And to this house some eighteen years ago he had brought the other two most important and precious people in his life: Julia and Nicole, both of whom he loved with the intensity and devotion of a man who had once loved and lost; then, when he had almost given up all thought of happiness, found love again.

He just hoped his very stable boat wasn't about to be rocked...not after all these years...

A pair of warm arms slid around his waist and Julia's face

132

appeared, reflected in the darkening window beside his own.

'Why so pensive, lover?' she asked, her voice still English to the core, with only the faintest trace of an acquired American accent.

Ryan gave a tight smile. 'Just thinking.'

She studied his reflection in the glass: his face older and more weather-beaten than when she had first known him, but handsome still, the incredible sapphire eyes un-faded by the years, the tall body still lean and broad shouldered, although the silver blond hair that once grew thick and straight was now a pure shinning white; shorter than in the 'sixties; no longer shaped to flop artfully across his brow by a Jermyn Street barber but even a little unruly. Like Ryan himself, she thought.

'Finished looking'?' he asked, turning to wrap his arms around her, 'not that I mind -don't get all that much attention from the ladies these days.' He looked down on her. 'You know, your daughter gets to look more like you every day...pity she doesn't have your cool head. Not that yours was ever that cool, you always were a might sassy for your size.'

Julia said tersely. 'At the moment my daughter is one very big pain in the neck.'

He raised his eyebrows, his eyes sharpening.

'She been on at you, too?' he asked, his mouth suddenly ominously tight.

Julia thought, *This is where I walk very carefully indeed.* Aloud she said, 'Uh, huh, wanted to know – in the most casual way of course, if I'd ever visited Hampshire – and she wasn't talking about New Hampshire either!' Julia's tone was light, but her eyes were troubled. Talk about walking on eggshells, she thought. 'I saw how you both looked when you came back together from the stores earlier and guessed she'd tried questioning you as well; you had your stony stare well in place and your face shut tighter than a clam – and she was mad as hell. I suppose she told you about the woman she met in Joe Lyons just before she flew home?'

'Yeah,' she felt the tension in his body like a steel spring, ready to snap and deliberately made herself relax even more. She knew her man: he was ashamed, still haunted by an old guilt and the last thing he needed was to be forced into a corner by Nicole. If her stubborn daughter didn't let the whole subject of Sophie Nicholls drop – which she wouldn't –and Ryan keep his usual stony silence, there would be the most almighty chasm open between them which might never again be crossed. She said quietly, 'Ry, you have nothing to feel guilty or defensive about. You did what you felt was the right thing...what

133

both you and Geoffrey agreed, and Sophie seems to have grown into a well-balanced individual, so why the angst?'

'Because I don't want to talk about it; I don't want to let Nic into that part of my life...it's gone, kaput. Why should I rake it all up again....hell,' his mouth twisted, 'I spill it all to her – and it would have to be all – and in her eyes I'll be just another randy GI who got himself laid and lit off home leaving some dame to pick up the pieces.'

'That isn't so and you know it. Nic is no wide-eyed prissy little madam who'll hold up her hands in horror...and Ry, you owe it to yourself now to see this through. Stop feeling guilty; take it out, look it all square in the face...for God's sake don't let it fester right up to the grave.'

She took his face between her hands, shook his head gently. 'It's time to let go, lover...and I have a feeling my nosy daughter may have done us all a favour.'

For a long moment he stood tense and still, then gave one of his short, defeated shrugs. 'Yeah,' he rested his forehead against hers. 'You're right, Goddammit! I'm sorry...I didn't expect it and I just brushed her off like she was a nosy kid...couldn't have done anything worse, could I?'

Julia smiled. The battle was at least halfway over; he wouldn't go back but she'd bet he'd give Nicole a rough time before he really let go. She said cautiously, feeling her way, '*Could* it just be coincidence? Sophie isn't such an uncommon name, after all.'

He raised his head and gave his wry smile. 'It is when used alongside Hawksley and Hampshire. I can't remember the name of the guy she married; I only heard it once and I was a bit too strung out at the time to take much notice, but the timing is right and Hawksley is a mighty small place to throw up a couple of Sophie's around the same age.'

'What are you going to do? It's over a fortnight since Nicola came home; she must have brooded over this and been working herself up to start talking – she even turned down that assignment to Chile, so the problem won't just go away now.'

'I know...but what the bejesus started her poking around the life of some complete stranger – and more to the point, what made her think *I* might be interested in her mystery woman?'

Julia narrowed her eyes. 'She and Joel spent a long time getting from Logan to here,' she said slowly, 'maybe he can answer that one.'

'Oh, no,' emphatically Ryan shook his head. 'I'm not about to waste my time asking him...be about as successful as tryin' to open a

134

clam with a toothpick.'

They were both silent for a few moments; behind them Ella gave way to the Carpenters and *We've Only Just Begun,*' Ryan relaxed; she felt the tension flow out of him. He chuckled 'I wish!' he said.

They began to sway together, then to dance; through the alcove and into the kitchen, his hands on her hips her arms around his neck. 'Beats the hell out of head banging,' he murmured, 'makes you glad to be old!'

'Not that old,' she said and pulled him closer.

They were still dancing when Joel took the steps from living room to kitchen in one leap, saw them clasped together and recoiled with an exasperated 'Jee-sus – and in the *kitchen?*'

'Yeah, you need a wood floor to dance,' Ryan's head was against Julia's, his eyes half closed. 'You want something?'

'Wondered when supper's gonna be. I'm starving.'

Without moving her head from Ryan's shoulder Julia said, 'You always are but at damn near thirty you should be able to get your own...this is Bracket Sound, Connecticut, not a luxury yacht in the Med.'

'Yeah, yeah,' Joel began opening and closing refrigerator and cupboards in search of instant gratification and failing to find anything to his liking said, 'Think I'll go join Nic down at Jake's Oyster Bar.'

Ryan raised an eyebrow. 'She didn't say she was figuring on dining out.'

Joel grinned. 'Probably stay out till midnight. She's well hacked off with you about something, dad.' He dropped a kiss on Julia's head, punched Ryan lightly on the shoulder. 'See you later; have fun...' he stopped at the hallway to call ''Most forgot...I'm off tomorrow afternoon...meeting Samuelson and the boat on Long Island, so Nic'll be all yours to sort out...if she doesn't take the next train to Timbuktu!'

Ryan watched him go. 'Cheeky bastard,' he said without censor. 'Seems like you and me can look forward to a peaceful evening, honey...we do have supper, I hope?'

'We do, so if you'll just let go of me I'll do the housewifely bit over a hot stove...*if* you promise to think hard about levelling with Nicole. Maybe it really is time everything was out in the open.'

'Yeah, OK.' He was grudging. 'I guess maybe you're right.'

'I always am,' she said and kissed him, a nice lingering kiss and he returned it in kind, so it was quite some time before they got supper on the table.

CHAPTER 20

Bracket Sound, December1983

'Dad, I need to talk to you; I really do.' Nicola stood on the jetty looking up at Ryan where stood on the deck of the *Dancer*.

'You do, do you?'

Her heart sank at the famous stony stare. "Frighten the bejesus outta you" Joel always said...So that was going to be the way of it. She set her chin. 'Yes I do. Can I come aboard?'

'If you must, but don't expect me to be pleased about it...I've a lot to do here; been out fishing with Joel these past few days so she needs a good hose down – like me she's getting old.' He walked back along the deck as she climbed on board. 'Better come below – I suppose you'll want coffee.'

She followed him down into the spacious cabin, very traditional with oak, folding table, red upholstery on the banquettes and shinning brass fittings. In silence she sat watching him fill the percolator and reach for the coffee jar before she said abruptly, 'Sorry about yesterday...I was out of order.'

'Sure you were.' He measured out the coffee, lit the stove, put the metal pot to heat then sat down opposite her and leaned his arms on the table. 'OK, guess we'd better have it all out in the open...I don't want to, mind, and I'm pretty sore about you wanting to rake over my past, which I figure is my business and not yours.' His eyes were still flinty but he gave that tell-tale hunch of the shoulders that told her maybe he wasn't as mad as he looked. 'Your mom thinks I should do this and I said I would. So say what you've got to say and I'll do my best to level with you.'

'This woman I met in London,' she began hesitantly, 'this Sophie Nicholls; she was an absolute ringer for you; I didn't make the connection at first...thought she might be someone in the news and I'd seen her picture somewhere. Then on the flight home I got to thinking...' She paused examining her nails for a few moments as though they might hold some inspiration, then gave a deep sigh. 'See, if she'd been twenty or so years older she'd have been so like you she could have been a twin, but I knew that was really crazy thinking, so then I started on figuring out her age and you being in the UK during the war, and that's when I got the notion she could have been your daughter.'

He said tersely, 'That's a mighty big supposition to make on the strength of a physical likeness. Nordic folk have itchy feet and there are an awful lot of them in the world with my kind of looks... I guess there were also quite a few of them bumming around the UK during the war.'

She said stubbornly. 'No one else I've ever met has eyes like yours; when she laughed they lit up, just like yours, and when she smiled her mouth went up at one corner...' She stopped and bit her lip. 'Don't be angry with me for spilling all this, but I've thought of nothing else since I left London and my head feels like it'll bust open like a ripe melon if I don't find some answers soon.'

'I'm not angry – well, guess I am some. I'm just...' he hunched his shoulders again; gave his wry smile, 'just figuring the best way to begin and not wanting to begin at all.'

There was a long silence. The coffee percolator began to gurgle and hiss; he got up to fetch mugs and a tin of sugar. 'No cream – you'll have to take it black,' he set the pot on a trivet between them and seating himself again leaned his arms on the table. 'OK,' he said, 'you asked for it, so here we go.'

'Our B17s were based in Hampshire, at what was formerly an RAF bomber station we re-named Falcon Field. Christmas nineteen forty-one we threw a party for the local kids. There were two villages near the base: Stratton Lay was a tiny place – the folk there called it a hamlet, it was closest to the airfield so we mostly drank at the pub there, but Hawksley was bigger and as it was the one with a village hall we held the party there. That's when I first set eyes on Claire de Lacy.' He paused to pour the coffee and push a mug across the table to her. 'She came early to fetch her son, Rupert from the party – around seven he was then –and she kind of fell through the door into my arms. Can't say it was love at first sight but it sure lit a spark between the two of us. She said she expected we'd meet again as her mother-in-law was planning a big New Year party and inviting all the crews from the base who were free to come.'

He sat for a few moments gazing into space before continuing. 'Before that happened we flew a pretty tough mission to bomb some marshalling yards in France and the old *Boston Babe* took a lot of damage; my bomb aimer, Scotty, got hit in the leg and passed out just short of the target and we got back home on a wing and a prayer. Scotty was taken to what they called the Cottage Hospital in Hawksley overnight; I remembered Claire said she was a Red Cross nurse there so I went to visit him hoping I might see her again.' He took a long pull at his coffee and gave a reminiscent grin. 'It had to be Fate...she was there alright; I saw her home and at the party her mother-in-law threw that New Year I danced with her half the night and almost got to kiss her...but not quite!'

Nicole grinned. 'So being you, you had to go on trying?' she ventured and he returned her grin.

'Yeah; I went on trying. Home for Claire was a darn great 17th Century manor house just outside Hawksley village and about a mile and a half cross-country from Falcon Field. She lived there with her boy Rupert, her ma-in-law Marion de Lacy; an old tartar of a nanny and a sweet lady, Mrs Buckley, who was the housekeeper. Seemed Claire's husband was a regular army officer out in North Africa...I found out later he was quite a lot older than Claire, a bit of a bastard and a womanizer and the marriage was not a happy one. Anyway, I had some leave after the New Year and helped out on the estate when they were logging; after that we got to meeting quite a bit. When I wasn't flying and she was on duty I'd walk from the base through some woodland and wait for her at an old gate at the bottom of their big meadow and walk her to the hospital. Then there was the day we first went riding...'

Again he paused to take another pull at his coffee. 'Geoffrey, her husband, had a big black hunter – Sampson...gee, but he was a great ride! One day we rode out into the New Forest: Claire on her mare Dolly, me on Sampson. That forest has a lot of open heath and when we reached it she stayed back while I let him go...and boy, could he go...' he smiled reminiscently. 'That was the day I first got to kiss her, and soon after that we became lovers.

'We were flying missions pretty regularly then, right through nineteen forty-two, so whenever we got to be stood down the air crews would get a forty-eight-hour leave pass; then I'd go up to London with Claire, to a quiet little hotel in Bloomsbury, where despite the German raids we could make our own little heaven away from prying eyes at Hawksley. Marion de Lacy was very fond of Claire and I guess knew pretty well what her son was and figured the marriage was already in trouble; but she didn't want to stir any village gossip any more than we did and always turned a blind eye.'

'But you must have made waves,' Nicole interrupted, 'people, especially in small villages know everything that goes on – hell, from what I remember of my grandpa's place in Devon, folk there would know if a sparrow farted!'

'True...I guess maybe most everyone did know, but they never let on...Geoffrey told me years later that the whole place closed around

Claire to protect her...and Sophie.'

'Don't get ahead of yourself, dad.'

Ryan leaned back, briefly closed his eyes. 'It's a long story, and complicated – and I want you to understand why I never went back. This wasn't some cheap affair, you know; we were just crazy for each other; so much in love; knowing it could end in a moment; that I could be shot down, or a bomb fall on us both in London...that Geoffrey could come home at any time. I wanted her to leave him when the war ended and come back here with Rupert; she said Geoffrey would never allow her to take the boy away...and that was true; the law in England at that time was pretty archaic; divorce was rare and no matter how unfaithful a husband might be, the law would have been on his side, not his wife's. I knew she couldn't leave Rupert behind, neither could I. By then I was very close to the boy...I guess I'd taken the place of the father he scarcely remembered. Going without him just wasn't an option, so it was *impasse* all round.'

Odd, he thought, as he told his story to Julia's daughter, that after all these years of silence it didn't hurt the way it used to; the ache in his heart that was always Claire, despite his love for Julia, had eased a little. Not gone entirely, he knew it would never do that, but fading into grateful remembrance.

Nicola's eyes never left his face as Ryan talked on; telling about those last few hours spent with Claire before he flew his final mission over Germany in nineteen forty-three. How they had been badly shot up over target, with the Fortress losing power and height as they approached the French border, unable to free the landing gear. How, with half his crew dead and the rest bailed out on his orders, Ryan himself was left in the shattered cockpit, his left foot trapped beneath a mass of twisted metal; then his crash landing on a ploughed field and miraculous rescue from the Fortress by French partisans minutes before it exploded.

'They'd been out cutting telephone wires and German throats and happened along at the right time for me – pretty tough guys they were: they hauled me out, busting my ankle in the process, but at least I was alive.' He paused, shook his head in remembered disbelief. 'The French civilians were incredible – when you remember that as the Germans began racing through France in 'nineteen-forty their army gave up, almost without a struggle, it's unbelievable to realise that in all those years of occupation, with the brutality of reprisal hanging over them if they stepped out of line, the French people as a whole never gave in. Now these guys took me to a farm where the son had been shot the night before while he was out sabotaging rail lines with the others. They'd brought him home and buried him under a barn, otherwise if the Germans came searching and found a corpse riddled with bullets the rest of the family would have been shot for supporting the Resistance. Without any messing those parents took me in, dyed my hair brown and when the Germans did come the next day, passed me off as their dead son, who'd had an accident with a tractor, was concussed and with a busted leg. Later the old man made me crutches and I hobbled around doing an impression of a farm hand until a platoon of British soldiers marched in eight months later. A couple of weeks after I was on my way home.'

'And you never let Claire know you were still alive?'

He heard the accusation in her voice. He said tiredly, 'No. I knew I'd have been posted as dead. Those of my crew who escaped would have reported I was trapped and never made it out of the Fort.' He shrugged; an old, familiar, what-the-hell shrug. 'I could have got word I was alive…the Resistance were very good at getting news of survivors back, but I had plenty of thinking time, Seemed to me that if I stayed dead Claire would never be faced with choosing between her son and me. I knew Geoffrey had been wounded and was already on his way home when I crashed, I figured with me dead Claire might be able to pick up the pieces and make some kind of life with him.' He paused and ran a hand through his hair. 'You see,' he said softly, 'I didn't know about the child; not then.'

They sat in silence for a long time, each mulling over their own thoughts…Ryan putting off the moment which would bring all the old anguish flooding back; Nicole, watching his sad, spent face was ashamed now of starting all this raking up of his past. Eventually she said hesitantly. 'I'm sorry, dad. You don't have to go on…'

'I think I do,' He raised his head, his eyes suddenly very straight and clear.

She gave a wan smile. 'OK, then. I'll make some fresh coffee.'

'I finished my war in the Far East and when I finally got home I was in a bit of a mess.' He sat back, took a sip of the fresh, hot coffee. 'I made a hasty marriage to Ellie, the girl I left behind, who loved me more than I loved her. She desperately wanted a child but miscarried a half dozen times before she made it full term with Joel. She was always a little flaky and suffered post-partum depression after the birth and never really recovered from it; it got worse in fact and ended with her most probably taking her own life, the year before I

140

went to the UK and when Joel was only a nine year old. Might have been an accident, might not – she was found drowned in the river after wandering off from the Psychiatric clinic she was in. So when I got the chance to go to England for a year, I grabbed at it...mostly to get Joel and me away for a while from Bracket Sound and the gossip; partly with the notion I might take a trip to Hampshire some time and find out what happened to Claire...not to see her; just have a look around; check if she and Geoffrey were still at the manor; how Rupert was doing. So a few weeks after we settled in London, I went down to do a spot of reconnaissance and discovered the Manor was open to the public at five bucks a throw. Guess the tax boys were fleecing them as they were everyone one else post-war – on both sides of the pond – and the de Lacy's were feeling the pinch. Any road, I figured the family wouldn't be around with a load of tourists tramping the place and took a chance...' He gave a sardonic grin. 'Oh, boy, did I get it wrong!'

'You found Claire?' Nicole was wide-eyed.

'No,' he said, 'Geoffrey found me.'

'Oh, my *God*!' she leaned forward. 'What happened – did you fight?'

He eyed her dispassionately. 'Nic, you are such a damn' drama queen...of course we didn't fight. I'd wandered off to have a look around the grounds and found Sampson grazing the stable paddock...' he smiled, 'he was real old by then but he sure remembered me. I'd stood talking and stroking him for a while, when guess who turned up? – and in a wheelchair – I was...' he stopped and grinned. 'The English have a word for it, don't they?'

She laughed out loud. 'Yeah – gobsmacked,' she said, 'you were gobsmacked!'

'I sure was.'

'And?'

'Nothing; I kept my nerve...chatted a bit; passed the time of day. See, I knew who *he* was alright because his portrait hung in the hall back in the time when I was around and he hadn't changed all that much, but I knew he couldn't know *me*. It was only when I was leaving and he said, "Nice to have met you at last, Mr Petersen," I realised I'd been found out – I tell you, I lit out like a cat out of hell to my car, picked up my things from where I'd stayed overnight at The Bull in Stratton Lacy, and high tailed it straight back to Chelsea.'

'Then, how d'you think he knew your name?'

He hesitated, pulling at his lower lip. 'I found that out when something else he said that at the time made no sense, sent me back to

Hawksley again a few weeks later...'

Suddenly he was exhausted; talked out. He raised a hand in protest as she bent forward eagerly, another question hovering on her lips. 'Sorry,' he said. 'I can't do this anymore right now. I'm bushed.' He forced a smile. 'Joel leaves in an hour or so and I don't want to see him off looking like I heard the Sox just got hammered again.'

Reluctantly she gave in. 'Sure, but you won't chicken out of telling me the rest when he's gone, will you?'

Ryan stretched, easing his back. He said cryptically, 'Well, sweetheart, I guess that kind of depends on how I'll be feeling later on...'

CHAPTER 21

Bracket Sound, December 1983

Joel, who hated being seen off by his family at airports, ships, trains or even bus stations, because he said it made him feel all the ghouls were gathering to say a final goodbye in case anything he was on or in crashed or sank. He liked his farewells quick, painless and from his own doorstep. As Ryan had over the years made more farewells himself than he cared to recall he could sympathise, so when the cab arrived at the door that afternoon and Joel's remarkably small amount of luggage was loaded, he sent his son on his way with a quick hug and a 'take care of yourself, fella,' while Julia, equally well schooled in farewells, kissed him briefly and said to remember to write.

Nicole gave a casual wave, told him to watch out for any gold-diggers who might be lurking in the Hibiscus bushes then watched the cab drive away with, her mother noted, an unusually wistful expression on her face, which made Julia wonder again if the reason the drive from Boston to home had taken so long was because they'd stopped off somewhere to talk…and a pretty long talk at that. She also wondered how much Joel, who even as a child had been an equal, even sharper observer of people and events than her daughter, remembered of their time in England. Although as she commented later to Ryan after Nicole had disappeared up to her room with a too casual; 'Catch you later, dad,' Joel would not have encouraged her to put her pretty little nose into anywhere he didn't think it ought to go.

'Oh, sure,' Ryan replied, 'you can bet she tried to pick his brain – and get him on her side… won't have done her much good, 'though, or she wouldn't still be hassling me.'

He appeared relaxed as usual, stretching his legs toward the stove and leaning his head against the back of the couch where they sat together in the den. Julia wasn't fooled. She turned her head toward him and asked gently, 'Did she give you a hard time of it this morning?'

'Uh, huh…but we haven't finished yet. I chickened out of the worst bit; I was bushed and told her she'd have to wait 'till Joel had gone.' For a few moments he stared unblinking into the fire then turned to take her hand. 'I know what you're thinking. You don't have to hurt for me,' he said.

Julia smiled. 'Someone has to, and it might as well be me.'

143

He raised her hand and put it to his lips. 'Was I right to let Geoffrey talk me into staying dead for Sophie…let sleeping dogs lie?'

'I don't know, lover…if it had been me, I don't think I would have had the strength to walk away as you did…not after hearing what happened to Claire and Rupert, then seeing your daughter for the first time as a young woman.'

He closed his eyes. 'Gee, Julia, but she was beautiful, wasn't she? I hope she's been happy and the guy she married has been good to her.'

'Would you go back again?'

'Not sure, I might if I thought she knew the truth – but how could she? Any road, dead men don't walk back into their daughter's lives after near on forty years.' He looked at his watch, leaned to kiss her lips and stood up. 'Time one daughter at least knows the whole score,' he said, then added, 'You might want to think about gettin' the arnica and band aids out while we're gone.'

They walked along the shore together, away from the small harbour where the boats rode at their moorings; the late afternoon breeze sending the water slapping against the hulls and stirring them into an uncoordinated sideways dance.

Although Nicole was just busting to ask more questions, something about the look on Ryan's face made her hold off and wait for him to talk in his own time, but he was in no hurry, just kept walking at his steady, long-legged pace. Then just as she was beginning to think this was the dumbest idea and she'd have to kick-start him he spoke.

'It was in late November when I returned to Hawksley; I waited 'till Julia had taken you, Joel and Hannah to Devon for the weekend before I drove back and put up again at the Bull in Stafford Ley. Eddy the barman had seemed the sort of guy who'd know pretty well everyone's business, not only in his own village but probably a fair amount about Hawksley folk as well, so I thought I'd tackle him first. You see there was something Geoffrey de Lacy said to me that first visit that just didn't make any kind of sense.'

He took both hands out of his pockets to rake his fingers through his hair. It was such a familiar gesture that she couldn't help smiling; whenever he was unsure, or frustrated, which really wasn't all that often, it was always his hair he punished. Her mother said it was a wonder he still had a thick thatch and not gone bald before his time.

'We were doing the idle chit-chat,' he continued at length, 'me trying to be casual but friendly and wondering how to get away from

144

him, when I made some remark about my son being at the demanding stage and he said...I can tell you his exact words...he said, "There you have the advantage of me. I don't have one of those, demanding or otherwise." Ryan thrust his hands back into the pockets of his pea jacket. 'Which was just plain crazy, because I knew damned well he had a son, so...' he turned, gave her a faint rueful smile. 'I just had to go back and find out.'

'Of course you did.' Encouraged by the smile she put an arm through his, 'and I suppose your friend Eddie told you.'

He said baldly, his normally warm voice suddenly harsh. 'Oh yes, he told me...Geoffrey was quite right; apparently what he had was a twenty year old daughter, but no son – or wife. Ten years after I last saw Claire and Rupert they were both killed in a car crash...the same one that put Geoffrey in a wheelchair for the rest of his life. He was driving but wasn't to blame; a lorry failed to stop at a junction and ploughed straight into the side of the Land Rover.' Suddenly his voice faltered. 'It was Rupert's last day at school and they were bringing him back to spend the summer vacation at Hawksley before he started University. He was just eighteen years old.'

'Oh, God, dad,' Nicole was aghast. 'I'm so sorry...*shit!*' She shook his arm, her eyes filling with tears. 'I'm such a bitch. I should never have started this...Joel told me to leave it all alone.' And she began to weep in earnest.

'Hey, hey,' Ryan's arms were around her. 'You don't have to beat yourself up...it was all a long time ago...' He put a hand under her chin, lifted her tear-stained face. 'I've lived with it for 'most twenty years and only aired it once to my ma, and yours, so maybe it was time to let it all out again.' He dived into his coat pocket and offered a handkerchief, 'Come on, cupcake,' he coaxed, 'the end of the world is still a long way off –' then recoiled in exaggerated horror, exclaiming, 'Oh Jesus, Nic, blow your nose will you...you look terrible with all that yuk running down your face.'

She began to laugh, scrubbing at her face and blowing the offending nose vigorously. 'Oh, go on, go on: don't look at me...'

So he went on.

'I got pretty well out of it that day; I don't recollect much of what happened after Eddie told me they were dead. All I remember is walking to Falcon Field and sitting on the steps of the old control tower, thinking about all the people I'd lost over the years: my brother Niles, who was killed at Guadalcanal, and all the friends who'd died: guys I'd flown with and been close to. So I sat on those old stone steps and just kind of fell apart.'

145

By now the light was fading and he stopped walking, and turning began to retrace their steps. Hugging her arm to his side he went on, 'I meant to go straight back to London next morning, then decided I'd stay and have it out with Geoffrey.' He shook his head at the recollection. 'Gee, but I hated him for just being alive when they were dead...and I wanted to know about the daughter – Eddie said she was about to be married and I resented that the bastard had been so quick off the mark after *me* to have a daughter old enough to be married. I wanted to know if he'd made Claire happy, what their life had been like...and how the hell he'd immediately known who I was when we'd never so much as set eyes on each other. But before I tackled him I first wanted to go see their graves. So I went to the little churchyard at Hawksley...and that's when I really got the second biggest shock of my life.'

Nicole couldn't contain herself and burst out, 'You saw Sophie and knew she was *your* daughter, not Geoffrey's!'

'Yup; I sure did.' He looked down at her, his expression half amused, half rueful. 'I was standing looking at the headstones for Claire and Rupert and Marion de Lacy when I heard someone coming along the path behind me. I didn't want to risk getting into conversation or even having to say hello to anyone just then, so I stepped right back into the trees as a girl with her arms full of flowers came into sight. At first she had her back to me and a scarf over her head; then when she'd laid the flowers and turned to walk away, she pulled off the scarf and I saw her face...and that hair...' He stopped for a moment and took a deep breath. 'Jeeze, Nic, but she was the spitting image of pictures I'd seen of my grandma Petersen when she was a girl. It gave me such a shock; I just stood like a dummy, then before I'd recovered enough to move or speak, she was gone.'

Nicole said sadly, 'So you never saw her again?'

'Just once; on her wedding day a few days after that Christmas; Julia came with me. We kept well out of sight...but when Sophie came out of the church and stood on the steps, she looked straight across the churchyard to where we were stood in the shadow of a big old yew, and I swear that for just a second she looked me full in the face-'

'–and you still did *nothing*?' Nicole was incredulous.

He sighed. 'That's right – see, by then I'd had it all out with Geoffrey during one memorable evening when I stayed overnight; We both got plastered and more or less sorted things out and agreed it would have been both cruel and horribly traumatic for Sophie to hear the truth just as she was about to be married – in effect, to be robbed

146

of the father she knew and loved to have him replaced by some total stranger who'd never even known she existed until a few weeks before.'

He shrugged and spread his hands in a gesture of defeat. 'So I stayed dead to her and let Geoffrey walk her down the aisle and give her away...and it wasn't so bad after all. Like most of us he came back from the war an older and wiser man; he and Claire eventually made a good life together. She had been completely honest with him about our love affair and he knew it was my child she was carrying. When Sophie was born he accepted her as his own and was a great father. Sophie had been told right from the beginning, soon as she could understand, that Geoffrey wasn't her real father – that *he* was an airman who'd been killed in the war even before she was born, and as kids do, she'd just accepted it and got on with her life.'

Nicole's brow was creased in a puzzled frown. 'I get all that, but how in hell did Geoffrey know who you were the first time you met?'

Ryan really laughed then, throwing back his head, startling into flight a couple of gulls foraging along the shore. 'It was Rupert...that first summer when he turned eight I gave him a puppy and Geoffrey sent him a camera...just a little box Brownie, but soon as he figured how it worked he took pictures; dozens of them: of Claire, me, Marion, Mrs Buckley...everyone he could keep standing long enough to snap, and he put them all in an album...' He shook his head, still laughing. 'It was the first thing he showed Geoffrey when he came home!'

* * *

'How did it go?' Julia asked much later, when the house was quiet and they were lying in bed together.

'OK, good in parts.'

'A bit like the curates egg.'

'Yeah,' he was laconic, back to the old, familiar Ryan, the master of the one-liner – even the one word. Julia smiled into the dark.

'She won't leave it there, you know. Someday she'll go back – just like you did; just to get another look.'

'I know.'

Julia slid and arm about his shoulders, drew him closer.

'Did Sophie ever see Rupert's album?' she asked

'I guess not.'

'But she might have?'

'Yup, she might.'

Julia pinched him gently. 'Are you doing your John Wayne impression again?'

'Yes, ma'am,' he rolled over; pulled her into his arms. 'You like being Maureen O'Hara?' he asked.

She said lazily, 'Only if you promise to melt my bones, Duke.'

Ryan raised himself on one elbow, looked down at her. In the faint light from the un-shuttered windows he saw her eyes sparkle. He shook his head. 'Waal, ma'am,' he drawled, 'reckon I'd be a fool not to, but if I remember rightly, in that there movie he did kind of whack her pretty little ass first.'

'Don't get carried away,' she said, 'it was only a picture.'

'Yeah,' he said, 'so it was.' He smiled. 'I love you, Julia Petersen – and you sure do have a pretty little ass of your own'

'Music to my ears,' she murmured, 'don't stop.'

'I wasn't going to,' he said.

Quite a long time later she said sleepily, 'You've still got a pretty good ass yourself, fly-boy!'

'One of life's little bonuses,' he said.

CHAPTER 22

Hawksley Manor, Hampshire, New Year's Day 1984

Sophie put the tray laden with percolator, cream, sugar, cups and saucers on the low table before the fire and said, 'Help yourselves – and I'll have it black with one sugar!'

Ben uncoiled his long legs from his easy chair. 'Poor love; are you absolutely wacked?'

'Of course she is,' Dominic, momentarily leaving his search for new reading matter turned from the bookcase as Ben began busying himself with the coffee. 'So many men, and not another woman of the household in sight, what else would she be?' and he shot Sophie one of his teasing looks. She put out her tongue at him, flopped into the chair opposite Ben and with an audible sigh kicked off her shoes, Tucking her feet beneath her skirt she said. 'Our first Christmas and New Year without darling Bucky was bound to be hard...and I don't suppose she's seen much of the festivities while she's been nursing Ella.'

'I imagine the Essex marshes might be a touch dreary in winter,' agreed Ben, 'very inconvenient of her sister to slip on the ice and break an ankle on Christmas Eve!'

'Very,' Sophie agreed. 'It was OK while Charles and Caro were here, but tough going since they deserted us to see in nineteen-eighty four with their new granddaughter and her proud parents.'

'Looking on the bright side,' Ben handed her a coffee, 'we did manage to lose Xanda and Jamie to the bright lights of London for this New Year.'

'Yes, but only just,' she returned and giggled like a schoolgirl. 'When Jamie's car wouldn't start I thought we were going to be stuck with both of them after all.'

Ben said, 'It was quite something, wasn't it to see them all done up in their glad rags, taking off to pick up their Mayfair floozies in a mud-spattered Land Rover!'

Sophie raised a languid hand to her brow. 'Oh, the shame of it,' she moaned theatrically and both men laughed. 'Actually,' she confessed, 'I did rather miss them but a New Year party for mid-life adults only was very soothing and enjoyable...none of that leaping about and head-banging they go in for these days.' She sipped at her coffee, 'And it was tactful of our friends and neighbours to leave soon

149

after *Auld Lang Syne*...after any party I like a peaceful hour or so to wind down before I stagger to my bed.'

'Me also,' Dominic finally selected a book and came to join them. He poured his coffee, drowned it in cream and lounging back on the couch took a long luxurious sip. 'This should settle all the wine I have enjoyed this evening...soon I shall take this book to bed and read a little before sleep.'

Ben said rudely, 'if it's your chosen bedtime reading it's bound to be along the lines of *'How to grow champagne grapes in a Korean paddy-field.'*

'Nothing of the kind...an essay; some poetry – it is Sophie's book perhaps?' and he held up a slim volume with a faded design of vertical stripped Fleur-de-Lys on board covers. He sniffed it. 'Smells a little musty...it had fallen behind some others.'

Sophie yawned. 'One of those I read for my degree I expect...I must have bought dozens of them second-hand when I was at Oxford and they always seemed to smell a bit off. What is it, an anthology?'

'I think not.' He turned to the frontispiece. 'It is about someone called Wilfred Owen...and naughty Sophie...this you did not buy in Oxford! It is a library book – here, it says: *This book is the property of Hampshire County Libraries* and it is stamped with a date for return: *July 15th, 1959!'*

'How awful...just think what the fine would be by now!' Sophie laughed and held out her hand for the book. 'I suspect I had what Pru would call 'a willing forget' about returning it; when I was around seventeen I was in love with Wilfred Owen.'

She took the small volume from Dominic and opened it at the title page.

Her eye travelled downward, then back again to the title, and downward again, taking in every word in a kind of frozen disbelief.

This little, worn book she held between her hands, printed on flimsy, sub-standard post-war paper was unreal, impossible, the dates were wrong; the name was wrong...they had to be. With a tremendous effort of will she forced herself to read the typeface again:

First printed in the USA February 1953
This edition re-printed in England July 1955 by the Medici Press.

The War Poetry of Wilfred Owen
An essay and notes by
Ryan L. Petersen, BA. MA. PhD.

150

Professor of European Literature
Harvard University, Boston, Massachusetts, USA.

She slammed the book shut. She said aloud, 'This is ridiculous. There can't be two of them!'

Ben glanced back over his shoulder from where he had knelt to stir the fire, 'Two of what?' he asked.

When she didn't answer he turned around to look at her more closely; she was rigid, her face was paper white and her eyes looked huge and unfocussed. 'For God's sake, Sophie, what is it?' Alarmed he moved swiftly to her side to take the book from her; but she was gripping it so tightly he had to almost prise her fingers open before he could release it.

By now Dominic had come to squat beside him. Looking over his shoulder he said, 'It's only an old book...an essay and some of the guy's poems.'

Ben said grimly, 'There has to be more to it than that.' Sitting beside Sophie he opened the book and for a moment sat absolutely still, then, 'Oh, Christ, Soph,' he said and wrapping his arms about her rocked her as though she was a baby.

Dominic poured three brandies and brought them to the low table; he held the first out to Sophie, who by then was shivering violently. She took it, her teeth chattering. 'Just the thing for shock,' she said and tipping the glass swallowed the fiery liquid straight down.

When she'd finished coughing Ben took both her hands in his. 'OK,' he said, 'Now we all calm down and really think this through.'

'There's not much to think, is there?' Sophie asked, fighting to stay calm when what she wanted to do was let herself fall apart, possibly scream, certainly throw something. 'Except that my father isn't dead but very much alive – or he was in nineteen fifty-three. I remember the book: I was reading it the afternoon I heard Pru and Bucky talking about my mother and her American lover, and how the chaplain had come to say he'd been killed...That time George and Tom told me his name it seemed to ring a bell, but I couldn't figure why it should... hang on!' the vertical lines between her eyebrows deepened in concentration and she snatched up the book from the table. 'That girl – Nicole, she said something...' she stabbed her forefinger at the title page. 'Look at that: 'Professor of European History,' and in Boston – Ryan Petersen is *her* step-father.'

Ben said cautiously, 'Isn't that a bit of a long shot? The name *could* be a coincidence.'

She shook her head vehemently, '*Two* Ryan Petersens? both Professors, both living in Massachusetts, both in England around....' she closed her eyes; did a rapid calculation, '...I put Nicole Frasier about the late twenties and if she was around ten years old when he married her mother in England, that puts him here, in this country, about the mid-'sixties...' she opened her eyes wide. 'Ben, remember all the odd going's on around the weeks before our wedding – when my dad an Pru were so jumpy– when Rupert's album went missing and Bucky said some mysterious stranger had spent a night here? At the time you said it was probably an American who'd might have been here in the Air Force during the war and come back for a visit, and that dad had taken the album to show him.'

Dominic grumbled, 'I wish someone would tell me what the hell is going on!'

Sophie said impatiently, 'In a minute...Dom,' her eyes were intent on Ben's face and his look of dawning comprehension. 'It was *him*, wasn't it?

Ben nodded. He said slowly, 'And before then, in the churchyard that day you thought you were being watched – '

'– and under the yew tree the day we were married!' She gripped his hands tight. 'Ben, he didn't die in the war; he came back twenty years later looking for my mother ...'

'...and probably walked straight into Geoffrey!' Ben said.

* * *

They talked until Sophie's head was reeling. Dominic had to be told the whole story by Ben, and looked as bewildered at the finish of it as he had at the beginning. Eventually selecting another book from the shelves he retreated to his bed with the comment that he hoped it would all sound a little less like a most unlikely fairy story in the morning and thank God his own father hadn't come back to haunt *him*, which made even Sophie smile and call him a pragmatist with no sense of imagination.

After he had gone she sat with Ben into the early hours, her mood ranging from delight at having a living father and bewildered fury that he hadn't cared enough to find her years ago...what man, she asked despairingly would abandon his lover and her child and wait twenty years to sneak back, spy on her, and disappear again without a word?

'Perhaps one who didn't know he had a daughter?' Ben answered. 'After all, you were born some months after he was supposedly dead. Be reasonable, Soph; the guy could have been seriously injured...

152

been a prisoner...lost his memory...any number of things could have happened...and if he did come back in the 'sixties looking for your mother, think of the shock it would have been for him to find that along with Rupert she'd died all those years before and he'd never known...perhaps still gone on hoping they might be together again someday. Who could blame him for taking off again; he might have thought he'd brought enough grief to your family without horning in on your wedding at the last moment.'

Sophie looked at him mournfully. 'But it wasn't only Ryan Petersen, was it...dad knew; and Pru; they just let him go and kept the secret all those years.'

Ben said, 'I imagine it took a special kind of courage, and love, from all of them, including your real father to do that.'

'Well,' suddenly she sat up straight, 'we know how to find out what really happened and why don't we?'

Ben raised one quizzical eyebrow and she gave the first real smile he'd seen since Dominic had handed her the book.

'We find out in what part of the world Nicole Frasier is in at present,' she said, 'and have her lead us to Professor Ryan L. Petersen, of Harvard University, Boston, Massachusetts, New England, the United States of America, The World, the Universe, Outer Space...'

She took his hand and held it against her cheek. 'Rupert's Legacy,' she said, 'his Captain Pop – and my father.'

CHAPTER 23

New York, January 1984

'Where have you been, Frasier...I've had some dame bending my ear four freakin' times in the last couple hours asking for you.'

'So? Officially I don't work here anymore – just come to clear my desk and kiss all you guy's goodbye.' Nicole put down her to-go coffee and a bag with two donuts: one jelly, one cinnamon, before looking enquiringly across the news room at the shock-haired young man wearing a blue and white striped shirt, red braces and an aggrieved expression. 'OK, Kev, who's been calling, and where's the fire?'

'Some dame called Nicholls with a snooty Brit accent...talks like Audrey freakin' Hepburn...she left a number,' and he waved a yellow post-it. 'Come an' get it, but it'll cost you, buddy.'

'Get lost, moron,' Nicole moved like lightning, snatching the post-it to shouts of 'Hoo!' and a splatter of applause from the half-dozen other reporters scattered around the newsroom. Everyone knew that Frasier with her dander up could be interesting and on a freezing snowbound Saturday afternoon in early January, the news room was hardly humming with activity. Anything that might liven up the place was welcome.

Nicole gazed down at the short message – *"Ring me anytime, Sophie Nicholls"* beneath was a UK 'phone number. She felt her stomach segue and sat down abruptly. Placing the post-it on her desk she studied it for a moment, then reached for her coffee.

'How long since the last call?' she asked.

Kev tilted back on his chair. ''Bout forty minutes...she must be in some hurry...said to call back freakin' collect.'

Nicole looked at him with distaste. 'You got another adjective you could use, Kev?'

'Plenty,' he grinned. 'But you know you wouldn't like them either.'

Nicole glanced across to the glass partitioned editor's office, fortunately empty at present; not that that mattered; this was her last day in New York and the paper could stand one more transatlantic phone call without going bust...Taking her coffee and donuts with her and ignoring the chorus of "naughty, naughty" from her about-to-be-former colleagues, she crossed to the office and closed the door.

There was the usual long delay before she heard the ringing tone, which was almost immediately cut and a disembodied English voice said breathlessly, 'Hello – Sophie Nicholls.'

'Hi,' Nicole's own voice was a little unsteady. 'It's me, Nicole. How are you?'

'Fine...heavens, I didn't expect to have you call so soon. Some chap your end said he'd no idea when you might be back.'

'You were lucky to catch me; I'm off to Boston in an hour or two.' Nicole wrinkled her brow. 'The US is a hell of a big place – how did you find me?'

'It was Ben, my husband's idea to try tracing you through Reuters ...I must say they weren't all that helpful – kept me hanging around for days nattering on about personal confidentiality and security.' Sophie gave a low laugh, 'I mean do I sound like a terrorist or an assassin? They wouldn't give me your address or home telephone but finally agreed on your office number. I hope I haven't got you into any trouble.'

'No,' Nicole laughed. 'I'm leaving New York today and moving to a new job...reckon I've had all the war zones I want. Now I'll be a kind of roving correspondent in Europe for a Boston paper...you know: rioting French students in Paris; Neo-Nazi cells in Berlin...Russian spies under the bed; that sort of thing.'

'Oh, good...I mean, quite peaceful, really, compared with your previous brief.' For a moment Sophie fell silent and Nicole waited, wondering what this call was really about. She didn't have long to wait. Sophie Nicholls, she was to find, didn't hang around.

'Thing is...I've just discovered in a pretty dramatic way that the father I've thought dead for the past forty years is probably still very much alive and living in New England. Look Nicole,' her voice was full of concern, 'this may come as an awful shock to you and you'll probably think I'm crazy, but I think *you* may just be able to tell me how and where I can find him.'

Nicole sat down in the editor's chair and began to swing from side to side. 'Hey, Sophie, she said, 'I kind of think I could have a shock or two for you!'

Some twenty minutes later she replaced the receiver. Well, she thought and reached for her cold coffee and donuts; that had sure racked up the newsroom 'phone bill a notch or two by way of a farewell present. Maybe, she mused as she bit into the first donut, she'd rack it up a touch more and call home before she left the office...

* * *

Sophie put down the receiver and looked across at Ben where he stood by the fire, then at the twins, lounging on the couch, and lastly at Dominic, stretched out in an armchair, his long legs crossed at the ankle. She raised her eyebrows. 'Now you've all had a jolly good earwig, are there any comments?' she asked.

Ben grinned and levered himself off the over mantle. 'I gather she'd already worked out pretty well as much as you had, and now knows a hell of a lot more; but you could fill in a few details on the bits we didn't hear.'

Sophie went to him and put her arms around his waist. 'I told you she was a tough girl. Like me she'd started with working out how I looked so familiar, then when that penny dropped began comparing dates and times. Once started she just couldn't leave it alone and waded straight in with...' she hesitated, her eyes suddenly very bright, '...with my father. Eventually he told her the whole story. Obviously she could only give me the gist of things over the 'phone, but I have his address and she's going home to this place Bracket Sound this evening and putting him in the picture.'

Ben's eyes were intent on hers. 'And can I guess what *you* are going to do now?'

She smiled. 'You can.'

He said, 'I'm coming with you.'

'No, I have to do this by myself.'

Jamie said, 'You go for it, ma!'

Xanda said, 'If you change your mind we'll all come.'

Dominic waved a languid hand, as only Dominic could, 'Oh la, la, la – let Sophie do it her way – '

'Which she will, anyway,' interrupted Ben.' He bent his head and kissed her very gently. 'Pack two of everything, darling; I believe it's pretty damn' cold this time of year in New England.'

He sat on the bed watching her pack. 'Are you sure you don't want to warn him you are coming?' he asked.

'Quite sure; this is a face to face thing; having any kind of contact over the 'phone would be just too horrendous' Sophie paused in the act of folding a thick Arran sweater. 'The hotel is on somewhere called Beacon Hill and sounds very traditional and cosy – '

'It bloody should be at the prices they charge,' interrupted Ben.

Sophie ignored him and continued, 'I'll ring Nicole from there once I've got orientated and had a night's sleep... Ben, I *must* settle somewhere on my own to catch my breath and think before I make the journey out to this Bracket Sound...I couldn't bear to meet my father face to face in some damned anonymous airport lounge, or worse, just turn up on the doorstep...you do see that, don't you?'

'Yes, darling, I do see that.'

'And the hotel have been so helpful...I didn't realise one just doesn't find taxies waiting in line at the airport as we do, but they have promised to send a car to meet me.'

'OK. OK...but just get on with the packing, will you love, or we'll make Heathrow just in time to see the plane leave the runway...'

* * *

Sophie resisted the temptation to check her hand luggage yet again. Willing herself to relax she settled back into her seat on the BA jet. The journey didn't bother her; she'd flown many times before but never alone and never on such a mission as this.

In these last few frantic days, when so much previously shrouded in mystery had finally been laid bare, the past had receded into some cloudy lost land and she had thought of little else but this coming meeting: what she should say; what they would both say...or if they would even like each other – but no, she gave an inward smile. Liking, she thought, would not be a problem.

The stewardess was at her elbow, asking if she would like coffee and Sophie nodded and smiled her assent. She stretched a little in her seat, careful not to disturb the elderly woman beside her, who appeared to have drifted effortlessly into sleep minutes after take-off and clearly wasn't about to wake, even for the joys of in-flight instant coffee served in plastic mugs.

Sipping her brew, which wasn't all that bad; she'd had worse on short-haul flights, Sophie gazed out of her window. They were flying above the clouds in brilliant sunshine and the combination of blue skies, sun, the layer of white cloud beneath, made her think of lying with Ben in their wide canopied bed at Hawksley on just such a morning, and had a sudden, panicky, desperate wish to have him here beside her...she gave herself an impatient shake.

No use getting cold feet now, she admonished herself silently. *You wanted to do this alone, so get on with it....*

* * *

157

Bracket Sound, January 1984

Ryan snapped the lock on his canvas grip, slapped his jacket pocket to check his passport and flight tickets were in place then shrugged into his trench coat.

'Quite sure you want to do this alone?' asked Julia, handing him a checked wool scarf.

'Yup,' he took her face in his hands, framing her for a moment before kissing her mouth. 'Love you, Julia; shall miss you like hell. I guess I could do with a hand to hold, but...'

'I know – "A man's gotta do what a man's gotta do,"' she said.

He grinned. 'You seen that movie too?'

'Several times,' she said, 'it always made me laugh.'

'It would.' An impatient double toot sounded from out front; he grimaced and picked up his bag. 'That's Al...I'll be darned if he didn't see me away the last time I made this journey; only then Joel was with me and it wasn't snowing!' He kissed her again, hard, then turned and in a couple of long strides was through the door and out of sight.

She stood in the silent room in the cold light of dawn and listened to the car engine fade away into the distance. Her heart ached a little for her beloved flying off alone, but she knew that was the only way for him...and Nicola would be here tomorrow and Joel the following day, then they could all follow on together for what was beginning to look like quite some family reunion...

At Logan, Ryan said goodbye to Al, cleared security, checked his luggage through and took a seat at the loading gate. He hadn't long to wait before his flight was called and by 9am they were airborne. His stomach churned briefly. Now there was no turning back.

What sort of welcome awaited him, he wondered. How difficult would it be to communicate with a daughter he'd never met, and when neither of them had ever exchanged so much as a word.

Well, that's your fault, an inner voice jeered, *You didn't even have the guts to 'phone and say you were coming– just going to drop out of the clouds, are you and say: "Hi, kid...surprise, surprise, I'm your dear old dad..".*

He winced and closed his eyes and wished Julia was sat right here beside him so he could take her hand. Without her he wasn't complete.

* * *

Boston, January 1984

By the time Sophie had unpacked her overnight case it was quite dark. She stood at the window of her hotel room on the hill known as the Boston Heights and looked out across a city ablaze with lights. It all looked very big and strange and daunting. She felt very alone and rather scared, although she wouldn't have admitted that to anyone, even herself. When the diminutive young man who had carried her luggage to room 201 asked if she would be dining in the restaurant or would prefer to order room service, she'd seized on the opportunity to eat alone in her room rather than in an unfamiliar restaurant amidst a sea of strange faces.

The meal when it came was beautifully cooked and presented; after her long day she was hungry and ate her way steadily through from the oyster soup and steak to the multi-coloured ice cream and fragrant coffee. Eventually, replete and yawning mightily, she bathed and slipped into the king size bed to sleep dreamlessly until dawn.

* * *

Nicole was unpacking her hold-all when the 'phone rang. Swearing beneath her breath she scrambled across her bed to grab the receiver. 'Hi, Nic Frasier here,' she said breezily, 'this had better be good I've just got back from New York and haven't caught breath yet.'

'Nic, its Sophie.'

'Hey, Sophie,' Nicola settled cross-legged on the bed, her voice warming, 'great to hear from you...how is everyone?'

'Fine, I hope. Actually I wouldn't really know because right now I'm sitting in a hotel room in Boston and suffering from very cold feet.'

Nicola sat up straight. 'In *Boston?* What in hell are you doing there?'

'I flew in yesterday. I couldn't wait. Now I wish I was back home...'

'It might be a good idea if you were,' Nicola began to laugh. 'See, my dad will have arrived in the UK a few hours ago...*he* couldn't wait either!'

There was a long, stunned silence from the other end of the line before Sophie joined, somewhat hysterically in her laughter.

Julia walked into the room carrying a pile of clean bed linen and stared bewildered at her daughter as she lay across the bed, 'phone clamped to her ear laughing uncontrollably. 'What on earth is the

159

matter with you?' she asked.

Nicole looked up, tears of laughter running down her cheeks.

'Oh, ma,' she said, 'you are just never going to believe this...' with an effort she returned her attention to the 'phone. 'Stay right where you are, don't move a muscle...I'll be with you in an hour.'

She put the receiver down and turned to her mother, 'I hope you've got a call number for dad.'

'Yes, some pub we stayed at once before in the next village to Hawksley. He should be there by now.' Still holding the linen she sat down beside her daughter. 'Don't tell me – let me guess,' she said. 'Sophie is here and he is there...sounds as though the old saying "Like father like daughter" is big in the Petersen family.'

'Yeah,' returned Nicole, 'So is jumping the gun!'

It was decided that as arranged, Julia would wait for Joel while Nicole collected Sophie from her hotel, for she would surely be glad of some moral support for her return to the UK on the next available flight. Meanwhile Julia would call Ryan and put him in the picture before he had a chance to make his way to Hawksley Manor and a non-reunion with his absent daughter.

'Talk about a couple of nut-cases,' muttered Nicole as she hastily re-packed her bag and snatched up her car keys. 'And to think *I'm* the one he's always going on about being impulsive...' she planted a quick kiss on the photograph of Ryan and Julia that always stood on her dresser. 'You just wait, dad, I'll not let you forget this one in a hurry. From now on this will be good for years as a snappy answer to any jibes you might dare to make about *my* "impulsiveness"...

CHAPTER 24

Hawksley Manor, January 1984

Ryan sat in the bar of the Bull Inn at Stafford Ley and debated if he should or should not have a third whisky...or even a fourth. Perhaps not, he decided; maybe after lunch, God knew he had time to kill but getting plastered so early in the day might not be such a great idea. Anyway, if he did and Julia got a sniff of it she'd likely give him hell. Twenty years ago in this very bar he'd gone on a bender to end all benders and afterward when he was sober, promised her it would never happen again. No matter how rocky the road, or how tough life might have been since then, he had kept his word.

Once he'd got over the first shock of Julia's telephone call he'd had to admit it was all kind of funny...him crossing an ocean to see Sophie; her doing ditto to see him. This reunion, when it came, had better be good! In the meantime, what could he do with the next twenty-four hours or so until his daughter, indeed *both* his daughters arrived?

A boy of about twelve came into the bar with a lunch menu; Ryan took in the shock of fair hair, the freckled nose and wily countryman's eyes and put out his hand. 'Hi, you must be Eddie's boy...I knew your dad a long time ago. I was real sorry to hear about the accident.'

The boy gave an uncertain smile, shook his hand. 'I'm Eddie, too. Dad used ter call me "Little Ed", but now I'm just Eddie.'

'It's a good old English name. You look just like him.'

Eddie blushed and grinned. 'I know. I gotta get back to school now. Mum said to call her when you're ready to order.'

'OK, see you later.'

Ryan watched him leave, then finishing his whisky let his mind drift back to the night he had first heard that Claire and Rupert were dead, and the older Eddie had sat and drank with him and comforted him and spirited the bottle away before his guest was completely legless. That was the night, Ryan remembered, that he had walked to Falcon Field and wept for Claire and Rupert and all the other friends and companions who had gone before them...Now Eddie himself was dead, killed in a motorbike accident one winter's morning a few years back.

He roused himself, rubbing his hands through his hair...what was that line in "The Go Between"... "*The past is another country, they do things differently there.*"

And so it was, and so we did, he thought, but this was the here and now and it had been one hell of a long time coming. He'd have his lunch, then walk the mile or so to Hawksley and make the acquaintance at last of this Mr Ben Nicholls who'd married his daughter, and, according to Nicole, had the temerity to plant a vineyard in the long meadow where Claire had come to meet him over forty years ago...

* * *

As night fell Ryan sat once again in the familiar cosy sitting room which used in his time to be the study, a drink in his hand, the flames in the fire leaping, throwing into relief the five faces settled before it and thought about the days when just one person had waited there for him; thought too about that last night when they had snatched just one hour together here before he flew what was to be his last mission from Falcon Field: of Claire's desperate love making as if, like him, she had some premonition that this would be the last time...they had thrown caution to the winds and now he had a darned good idea of what, or rather who, had been the consequence of that frantic hour...

He looked around the circle of faces again...Ben Nicholls – who could find him anything less than agreeable: that open, boyish face full of humour, but with a firm mouth and jaw that promised an underlying strength beneath the easy charm. Not a man quick to anger, Ryan thought, but not one to cross, either – and those two tall young men, Ben and Sophie's boys, one dark, filled with a kind of restless energy, the other fair and placid with far seeing blue eyes. His heart caught a little...so like his own brother Niles before he had gone to war, never to return. Lastly, the whipcord thin Frenchman with his saturnine, *louche* looks...Ryan smiled to himself, he knew a woman magnet when he saw one and couldn't help wondering just how he fitted so easily into this household...his eyes drifted again, as they had ever since he'd entered this room this evening, to the photograph on the mantelpiece: a laughing Claire de Lacy and himself at the gate in the long meadow that led to Belstead wood.

Rupert's photograph. He could hear the excited little voice now..."*Oh do stand still, Captain Pop – and stop making mummy wriggle...*"

Ben watched Ryan watching them; the way his eyes kept returning to the photograph and divined some of his thoughts and feelings. He liked this new father-in law, liked the way he looked and talked: confident assured, although on this particular occasion he was probably neither – but in no way too confident, nor too assured; on the surface just a really nice, easy-going sort of chap, but pretty tough beneath. The kind who never used a half dozen words where one would do; who would invariably be at ease, whatever the situation or company. He wondered if Geoffrey had liked him and thought he probably had. There wasn't very much he could see to dislike – and, Lord, wasn't his darling Sophie just the image of him...maybe not so much now in the features, apart from those high cheekbones and amazing eyes, because Ryan was beginning to show his years.

It was more in the expression, a turn of the head, a laugh...even that shining hair, silver now but so like Sophie's blonde, always slightly dishevelled cascade, which had been the first thing to catch his eye all those years ago across a crowded room in Oxford, at some party for a chap whose name he could no longer remember.

When Ryan rose to take his leave Ben insisted on driving him back to the Bull Inn.

'I'll give you a call and come for you when Sophie and Nicole are on their way...that's if you'd like me to,' he smiled at Ryan's involuntary wry grin and added, 'unless you'd rather meet Sophie alone and in your own time.'

'I would, but if you let me know about when you expect them I'll walk over and work it out on the way.' He grinned again. 'Always did think better on my feet,' he said.

'Me too,' Ben drew to a halt before the Inn. 'I wish you'd stayed overnight at the Hall...there's plenty of room.'

'Nah,' Ryan swung himself down from the Land Rover, 'too many memories for that,' he said. 'Last time I stayed the night Geoffrey drank me under the table and I woke up with my eyeballs fried and a throat dry as the Sands of Iwo Jima...so thanks for the invitation but I'll take a rain check on that.'

He stood in the road and watched the Land Rover out of sight, then turned to enter the Inn humming, *"It's a lovely day tomorrow..."* under his breath.

Lovely, yes, but just a tad scary, too.

CHAPTER 25

Hawksley, January 1984

When Claire stepped from the train into Ben's arms she was exhausted, both physically and mentally. All right for Nicole, that seasoned traveller used to charging around the world and taking jet lag in her stride, leaping from the train as though she'd just got out of bed; she, Sophie Nicholls, forty years old and feeling every one of them was ready to lie right down on the platform and sleep like the dead.

'I was up at six, we took off from Logan Airport at eight in the morning,' she moaned piteously, 'we didn't clear Heathrow until after eight this evening and now it's almost ten-thirty...Nicole, how *can* you look so fresh and blooming after all that?'

Nicole grinned. 'Because I am pure in mind and body,' she said and Ben laughed and drew his wife closer into his arms.

'I know, darling, let's just get you home and you can crash for as long as you please.'

'He is still here, isn't he?' she asked anxiously as they walked towards the car, 'please tell me he hasn't shot off back to bloody Bracket Sound?'

'No darling,' he's at the Bull Inn at Stratton Ley and the last I saw of him he wasn't going anywhere.' Ben was at his most soothing, whilst trying, not very successfully to suppress his laughter. Poor old Soph, she really had had quite a time of it...

A little over an hour later she had eaten, bathed and was curled peacefully in the big old canopied bed at Hawksley. Her eyes already drooping in sleep she murmured, 'You are so lovely to come home to. If he's half as nice as you, he'll do.'

'He'll do anyway,' Ben said and watched as she drifted into sleep, and when he was sure that sleep was sound went downstairs to put a call through to the Bull Inn at Stafford Ley. Too bad if they were all in bed by now, he thought, but Professor Ryan L. Petersen needed to know that his daughter Sophie was home at last.

* * *

It was a cold, still morning with a pale sun just edging the grey clouds that were fast gathering above him. Ryan leaned on the gate, twin bars of cold seeping through the sleeves of his tweed jacket from the cold metal, his legs rapidly chilling despite his wool socks and heavy cord trousers. He wondered briefly if he'd read her wrong and she wouldn't know where he would be, then remembered the photograph on the drawing room mantle and knew his intuition was right. He could wait; she would come.

And she came at last, walking with her mother's swinging stride, in wool trousers and scuffed boots and worn sheepskin jacket, her bright hair moving on her shoulders as she came towards him. He straightened as she stopped a few feet away, hands thrust deep into her pockets, her face a mixture of uncertainty, apprehension and not a little bravado. Ryan felt his heart take up a slow, uneven thud. He straightened and swallowed hard. He touched the gate.

'What happened to the wooden fella that used to be here?'

She said, her voice a little unsteady. 'It fell apart, ages ago. I guess it just got old.'

'Like me,' he gave his lopsided grin and held out his arms. 'Hi, Sophie.'

'Hi, dad,' she said and went into them.

'I told myself I wasn't going to cry,' she said some time later, mopping her eyes with his handkerchief.

'Me neither,' he said, 'but when you've finished I'll have that soggy mess back for a piece...this guy is too old to be wiping his nose on his sleeve.'

Sophie leaned forward and wiped his eyes and nose as she had her sons when they were small boys. 'Let's walk and talk a little, shall we?' she stood back, considering him for a few seconds, then gave him back his own involuntary lop-sided smile. 'Oh, Captain Pop,' she said, 'you've an *awful* lot of explaining to do...'

So they walked and talked and filled in the gaps. She told him about finding Rupert's album after his death and how he had once taken her to Falcon Field when she was a little girl. and how she'd found the field again after so many years. And Ryan told how he had been shot down and hidden for months in France and not returned to Claire because Geoffrey would never let Rupert go and she could never leave him behind...

'So I stayed dead, and when I finally went back home I built a wall around me that kept Claire and Rupert in, and everyone else, even my mother, out,' he said. 'It took me twenty years, a girl named

Julia Frasier, a visit to a churchyard – and my first sight of you to want to start to demolish that wall.'

Sophie gave a little secret smile, 'It was you,' she said,' in the churchyard that day and later, at my wedding, it was you, under the trees and you looked at me...' she hugged his arm. 'Ben *said* it was you.'

'He was right...me and my lady...you'll like Julia,' he said, 'she's the reason I'm here...bullied the hell out of me to level with Nicole when it was the last thing I wanted to do.' Smiling he shook his head. 'I can't wait 'till we're all together...I like your Ben, by the way – and your boys. Hear one of them is going to fly....and hey, what's with the Frenchman – where does he fit in?'

She told him and her gave her a sideways look, 'Struck me he was quite a ladies man, even though there were no ladies present last night.'

'He is,' she gave a small secret smile that had him wondering. 'There was quite a lot of eye contact, not to mention a spot of footsie between him and your Nicole at breakfast this morning!'

Ryan gave a deep, growling laugh. 'She knows what she's doing around the guys,' he said, 'and if he keeps her from rushing off on any other half-assed assignments, he can have all the eye candy he likes!'

Talking, laughing, father and daughter walked on arm in arm, and as they reached the steps to the long back terrace where the wild thyme grew, the first fat flakes of snow began to fall.

Sophie stopped and lifted her face to Ryan's. 'You will come back...after this...you will come back, won't you?'

'I'll come to back to Hawksley in the summertime, this and every year,' he said, 'if you and yours will come to Bracket Sound every fall.'

'It's a bargain,' she said. Ryan brushed the snowflakes from her hair then kissed the top of her head and they walked together through the long French windows and into the little study where, on that last night before he was shot down and unknown then to either lover, Sophie de Lacy had begun the journey that forty years on had come full circle: to her father, to her new family, to the rest of her life.

Somewhere, out there, in the fading light and through the falling snow of that cold January day, a small boy's voice seemed to echo across a sunlit meadow:

"Oh do *stand still, Captain Pop..."*

166

By the same author

A Year Out of Time

A Year Out of Time is the story of one twelve year old girl from a "nice" middle-class background and a "nice" private school (where her mother hoped she might learn to be a lady) who, in the Autumn of 1940, finds herself pitched into the totally foreign environment of a small Worcestershire hamlet.

For the space of one year her life revolves around the village school and its manic headmaster; the friends she makes, notably Georgie Little the "bad influence"; the twee but useful fellow evacuees, Mavis and Mickey Harper, whose possession of an old pigsty proves the springboard to some surprising and sometimes hilarious happenings; and Mrs 'Arris, the vast and formidable landlady of The Green Dragon Inn.

In the company of Georgie Little she awakens to the joys of a new and exhilarating world: a secret world which excludes most adults and frequently verges on the lawless.

The year comes to an explosive end and she returns unwillingly to her former life – but the joyous, anarchic influence of the Forest and Georgie remains, and sixty years on is remembered with gratitude and love.

ISBN 978-0-9555778-0-2

Available from Sagittarius Publications
62 Jacklyns Lane, Alresford, Hampshire SO24 9LH

By the same author

And All Shall Be Well

And All Shall Be Well begins Francis Lindsey's journey through childhood to middle age; from a suddenly orphaned ten year old to a carefree adolescent; through the harsh expectations of becoming a man in a world caught in war.

Set mainly against the dramatic background of the Cornish Coast, it is a story about friendships and relationships, courage and weakness, guilt and reparation.—*The first book in a Cornish trilogy.*

ISBN 978-0-9555778-1-9

**Chosen as the runner-up
to the Society of Authors 2003 Sagittarius Prize**

"The author has succeeded to an extraordinary degree in bringing Francis to full masculine life. The storyline is always interesting and keeps the reader turning the pages. All in all it is a good novel that can be warmly recommended to anyone who enjoys a good read."
– Michael Legat

"Seldom do I get a book that simply cannot be put down. The settings and characters are so believable, the shy falling in love for the first time and the passion of forbidden liaisons written with feeling. Many of the sequences left me with a smile on my face, others to wipe a tear from my eye." – Jenny Davidson, The Society of Women Writers and Journalists Book Review

"A beautifully written novel. Eve Phillips' writing is a pure joy to read and her wonderfully graphic descriptions of the Penzance area of the Cornish Coast made me yearn to be there."
– Erica James, Author

Available from Sagittarius Publications
62 Jacklyns Lane, Alresford, Hampshire SO24 9LH

By the same author

Matthew's Daughter

Matthew's Daughter is the second book in a Cornish Trilogy and follows Caroline Penrose, as she returns from her wartime service in the WAAF to her father's flower farm in Cornwall.But once home she finds a number of obstacles and family conspiracies impeding her path to peace...

ISBN 978-0-9555778-2-6

The Changing Day

The Changing Day the final book in a Cornish Trilogy, begins in 1940, when a meeting between WREN Joanna Dunne and Navy Lieutenant Mark Eden is the start of a love affair that at first seems unlikely to stand the test of time. She is 22, single and an Oxford graduate; he is 36, married and in civilian life a country vet. She is attracted but not looking for romance, he is attracted but not looking for commitment and, as Joanna soon discovers, he is the black sheep of his family and has a very murky past.

ISBN 978-0-9555778-3-3

Available from Sagittarius Publications
62 Jacklyns Lane, Alresford, Hampshire SO24 9LH

By the same author

A Very Private Arrangement

When in the spring of 1934, fourteen year old orphan Anna Farrell is transported from a life of drab, penny-pinching, genteel poverty with her cousin Ruth, to the elegant, affluent Bloomsbury household of distant cousin Patrick Farrell, and his manservant, Charlie Caulter, she is at first blissfully unaware of the well hidden secret kept by the two men, until a meeting with the quasi-charming Madame Gallimard and her sons becomes the catalyst that threatens to tear her world apart.

Against the backcloth of WW2 and a diversity of places and people, with her beloved Patrick and Charlie to smooth her path through the inevitable pitfalls of first, second and last love, Anna matures from naïve young girl to confident young woman, well able to cope with the men in her life – and some of the women in theirs.

ISBN 978-0-9555778-4-0

Return to Falcon Field

Ryan Petersen, a professor of European Literature at a New England University, accepts a year's exchange lectureship in London. But in coming to England the cynical, detached Ryan has a hidden agenda: to find the woman with whom he had a passionate wartime love affair over twenty years before.

He returns to the now derelict airbase of Falcon Field and the nearby Hampshire village of Hawksley, to begin a journey into the past; one that proves both painful and inspiring as he re-discovers the man he once was, and perhaps could be again.

ISBN 978-0-9555778-5-7

Available from Sagittarius Publications
62 Jacklyns Lane, Alresford, Hampshire SO24 9LH

A Very Artistic Affair

The year is nineteen sixty-five. After twenty years of marriage Olivia, a forty-five year old wife and mother, discovers that her husband, Giles, has fallen in love with a young actress half his age.

Already feeling the first stirrings of discontent as the conventional and dutiful wife of her far from faithful husband, and conscious that the Swinging Sixties is rapidly passing her by, a humiliated and angry Olivia leaves the family home, moves from Hampshire to Devonshire, discards her twin-set and pearls image, resumes her earlier career as an artist, acquires her own occasional lover and copes successfully with her teenage son's burgeoning affair with a sculptor's daughter.

But as the months pass neither Olivia nor Giles find the separate paths they have chosen free from difficulty. There is confrontation, conflict and pain as events take many unexpected, sometimes tragic, and sometimes farcical twists and turns, before either can leave the past behind them and move forward into a new, and hopefully more peaceful, future.

ISBN 978-0-9555778-6-4

Available from Sagittarius Publications
62 Jacklyns Lane, Alresford, Hampshire SO24 9LH

By the same author

The Turning Point

Growing up is hard to do. Even at twenty two...

Landscape photographer Cassandra Chisholm is permanently hard up. She has an absent father in Paris and a not very satisfactory lover in Cornwall. When she agrees to take publicity photos for middle-aged author Michael Niven, the process of growing up begins to accelerate at an alarming rate.

Unrequited love; unwanted revelations about her past, and the frightening prospect of leaving her Cornish home, has Cassie arriving at her own personal Turning Point. Aided by her thespian friend Jono, she begins work at a London Arts Centre, until a series of romantic misunderstandings and family disruptions send her bolting around the Home Counties pursued by an irate Michael and her bewildered father. Ultimately it is left to Michael's own irascible octogenarian father Archie, whose many eccentricities include taking his pet ferret into battle on D Day and keeping a herd of politically incorrectly named pigs, to finally run Cassie to earth and restore peace and harmony between the warring parties.

More or less

ISBN 978-0-9555778-7-1

Available from Sagittarius Publications
62 Jacklyns Lane, Alresford, Hampshire SO24 9LH

By the same author

Feet on the Ground

Take one ex-professional soldier with one ex-wife, one delinquent teenage son, one cantankerous old manservant and one beautiful but neglected country house.

Add one strong-minded ex- PA, who has just lost both her job and her lover; toss in one hippy gardener with a colourful past, and one very large hairy dog with few social graces.

Deposit all on a gale-swept Cornish coast in mid winter; stir vigorously, then stand well back and see what human chemistry can do to your heart...

ISBN 978-0-9555778-8-8

Available from Sagittarius Publications
62 Jacklyns Lane, Alresford, Hampshire SO24 9LH